My Name Is Pink

VERONICA LANCET

Prologue

BIANCA

AGE SIXTEEN

"WIPE THE BLOOD off your face, kiddo." I turn my head to see Drew, my mentor, looking at me with a frown. He points toward my forehead, right above my eye. Folding the sleeve of my blouse, I dab at my skin, red liquid transferring onto the material.

"Done?" He nods with a grunt, shifting so he's looking toward the house.

"You shouldn't be here. You might get caught," he mentions, hands in his pockets and rocking on his heels.

"I was curious," I say, and I take a few steps to find a better angle. "I want to see what the fuss is all about with these parties."

"Like that?" He raises an eyebrow, his eyes traveling down my body with amusement. Having just finished an assignment, I'm in full gear. I'm wearing a full body-suit in black — black helps mask the blood — with my guns holstered, one on each thigh.

I shrug. "I just got curious." He shakes his head, knowing fully well that my moods dictate what I do — regardless of the consequences.

"Satisfy your curiosity quickly and go change. He has important guests tonight. Guests that might take an issue with the blood residue on your clothes."

I snicker at him and proceed to go even closer to the house. When I'm able to see through the window and right into the ballroom, I stop. I tilt my head, narrowing my eyes as I study the guests. My lip curls in disgust as I see people prancing about like paragons of virtue when I know how corrupt they are. My eyes follow a particular senator I'd heard has a penchant for brutal-izing his hookers. My fingers itch as they wrap them-selves around the handle of one gun. A click, and the wretch would be gone. I almost go through with it, but someone else catches my eye.

A young man strides in, engaging the senator in conversation. Whatever he's saying to him isn't good, going by the senator's sour expression. He looks abso-lutely pissed, and with a few huffed words, he walks away. That leaves the young man out in the open, and fully available for my perusal — and oh la la, is he fine. He struggles to hide the smirk threatening to over-whelm his features, and I find myself enthralled.

One more step.

I'm even closer to the window now, and I know I'm courting danger, my recklessness increasing by the second. But this . . . this man. I study him further, my eyes following his movements and watching his interactions with the rest of the guests.

It's odd. I've never noticed a man like this . . . like my entire body is humming with an unreleased pressure. I'm frustrated, and I know it's because that man isn't here, paying attention to me, touching me. I zone in on him, and the moment he raises his eyes, looking into the distance, my breath hitches. It's like he's looking at me, even though I know he can't see me. But I feel his gaze, the intensity of his eyes, and a shiver runs down my spine.

"Kiddo, time to go," Drew comments from behind me, but I put my hand up to silence him.

"What?" He frowns, coming to stand by me. I'm still focused on that wonderful male specimen, and I find that I don't care to divide my attention. "What are you looking at?" he persists, so I say the only thing that's on my mind.

"Him. I want him." I don't know who he is, but I know one thing.

He is mine.

And I'll do whatever it takes to make him mine.

Theodore Hastings, age twenty-four, and a recent Quantico grad. I'd found out everything about him — on paper. But who are you, Theo?

Who are you, really?

I smile to myself as I fold the sheet and place it back in the folder. I remove the photos the P.I. I'd hired had supplied, and I peruse them. Hazel eyes that sparkle with warmth draw me in, holding me captive. It's not only that he's attractive, with his short dark hair and his full, kissable lips. No, it's more than that. In his eyes, I see something I lack — empathy. I see everything I want to be, but cannot.

My fingers softly touch his face in the photograph. He's a savior. He volunteers at two homeless shelters and an animal shelter. He likes to spend his time helping people.

He's the exact opposite of me.

Hell, he probably puts people like me behind bars — the cold, unfeeling type. The ones who kill in cold blood and relish the sight of life leaving a body.

I've known who I was long before the ASPD diagnosis, and even then, I'd just shrugged it off and moved on. But now . . . now it might just prove to be a problem.

Because Theo would never willingly involve himself with a criminal.

I bet he goes for the shy, simpering type. The moment I think of him with another woman, a red haze covers my eyes. No . . . that can't happen. But I'm also smart enough to know he wouldn't be interested in someone like me.

I need to change strategies —.learn his habits and preferences and make myself the woman of his dreams. All while keeping all competition away from him.

My plan can't be completed overnight. I will probably need time to create another persona, and to infiltrate his world so seamlessly he won't ever suspect a thing.

Because I don't just want him.

I want to keep him.

Forever.

CHAPTER

One

BIANCA

AGE NINETEEN

"YOU CAN START." I nod at the woman as I take a seat. The chair is parallel to the bed, and this angle allows for perfect visibility. Raising my gun just a little so they can see I'm not kidding, I lean back and make myself comfortable.

The woman drops to her knees, her hands trembling as they struggle with the fastening of the man's pants. I roll my eyes at her obvious anxiousness and spare a glance at my watch. Vlad will not like this.

"Faster!" I snap, thinking I'd already wasted enough time with the threats. If she keeps this up, I'll have a furious Vlad on my hands, and all for nothing.

"Y-y-yes," she stammers and finally takes his dick out. Surprisingly, he's hard. Then again, given his age, he probably took something to help him out. I motion for her to continue.

She lowers her head, and opening her mouth, she takes him in. I narrow my eyes, trying to look at her technique. I'm busy observing when the door bursts open.

"B, what's taking so long?" Vlad groans as he enters the room, locking the door behind him. He takes one look at the bed, then his eyes find me before shaking his head.

"He was having a tête-à-tête with a prostitute," I shrug, pointing toward the mid-coitus couple.

"So?" He arches an eyebrow, hand on dagger as he playfully rotates it in the air. "What are you waiting for?" he asks, exasperated. I knew I should have been more succinct in my threats to get the action going faster. Vlad is not the patient type.

"Don't you see?" I stand up, coming around the bed and pointing toward the huddled figures. "This is my opportunity to learn from a professional. Miss . . ." I look at her.

"Abigail," she breathes out, her lip trembling.

"Thank you. Miss Abigail here was just about to demonstrate the act of fellatio."

We'd been ordered to assassinate the CEO of an oil company — Mr. Horace Bentham. I don't know if it had been luck or fate, but I'd got to him just as he was about to dip his wick in Miss Abigail. Now, I am not one to miss an opportunity when it's staring me in the face. Mr. Bentham would be dead, but only after I've assuaged my curiosity.

"A blowjob, you mean." Vlad rolls his eyes at me, swinging his knife around and making sure the guests understand the unspoken threat.

"Same thing." I wave my hand dismissively, and I take my seat once more. "Come, watch! You might learn a thing or two, as well."

"I'm fine," he replies drily. "You have ten minutes. No more. We need to hand in the proof that he's dead." He takes two steps and positions himself next to the windowsill.

I frown.

"Ten minutes? Is that how long sex lasts? I thought it was longer." I try to think back to all the magazines I'd read, but I realize none of them gave an explicit duration.

"B," he groans, bringing his hand up to massage his temples. "I don't know how long sex lasts, but we are on a mission. He should have been dead half an hour ago. You're taking a risk."

"Pretty please?" I bat my lashes at him, watching mild annoyance turn to defeat in one . . . two . . . Yes!

"Fine. But you owe me."

"Of course!" I beam. I know the rules. It's always quid pro quo with Vlad. We've been partners for three years now, and while our teamwork had been rather patchy in the beginning, forced proximity and a similar approach to life — or death, rather — made it easier to bond. We're in this together, and so we've learned to make allowances for the differences in our behaviors. You might say that temper-wise we are completely different, I'm rather indifferent to things, and tend to be cool, while Vlad . . . well, safe to say it's better to not find out.

I pull up another chair and place it next to me. Patting it, I motion for Vlad to join me. He shakes his head, muttering something, but relents and sits down.

It takes a little more urging to get Abigail and Bentham moving, mostly in the form of me waving my gun around and shouting some directions. But soon, we are back on track and Abigail is once again sucking him off.

I crane my neck, intently watching the movements of her mouth and tongue.

"She's focusing too much on that area. Is it more sensitive?" I nudge Vlad.

"For God's sake, B, how would I know?"

"Well, you have one." I roll my eyes at the obvious, but then another thought crosses my mind and I whip my head to regard Vlad suspiciously. "You do, don't you?" Considering his nonexistent love life . . .

"You're getting too personal and in my personal space." His hand comes to my forehead, giving me a flick that has me wince in pain.

"That hurt, douche," I mutter, keeping a distance between us.

Back to watching the couple, I tell them to switch positions and get to the nitty gritty. I already know Vlad won't stand still for much longer, so I might as well get to the highlight of the show.

Bentham is on his back and Abigail climbs on top of him, lowering herself onto his dick and riding him. From my vantage point, it looks rather . . . simple.

"Hmm . . ." I muse, bringing my thumb up and placing it under my chin. It can't be too hard.

So focused I am on watching Abigail's movements that I don't realize Vlad swiping the gun from my hand. I turn to him in time to see him aim at Bentham. Everything happens in slow motion as I open my mouth to scream no, before remembering I shouldn't draw any attention. The silencer on the gun ensures the shot is inaudible. I look in horror as a red circle appears on Bentham's forehead.

"You didn't!" I breathe out, my eyes widening at his audacity. Not only did he just ruin my show, but he also stole my fucking kill. "Vlad. You . . ." I purse my lips, holding myself together. It won't do good to explode right now. Not when Abigail is wailing by Bentham's dead body.

"You." Vlad points to Abigail, his voice dull and emotionless.

Really?

Vlad has certain triggers that make him . . . volatile. The easiest way to recognize the signs that he might succumb to his malady — whatever that is — is to watch his voice. He's learned to perfect an amiable, sarcastic tone, mostly so that people will find him harmless and normal. He's anything but, though. And when his voice becomes cold . . . I shudder instinctively, my eyes going to the window. We're on the fifth floor. I wonder how many bones I'd break if I were to jump. I mentally remember the layout of the hotel and the outside architecture, hoping there's at least something to whichI can hang on. One thing's for sure: if Vlad goes mad, I'm out.

"Get back on top and fuck him," he commands. I tilt my head very slowly, and I see that his eyes don't have a glazed look — yet. Ok, maybe he's not that gone.

"But . . . he's dead," the girl whimpers, trying to cover herself.

"I don't care," Vlad continues. "Now!" His voice booms, and Abigail finds herself unable to refuse.

Bentham's dick is still hard, even though his eyes are blank. Abigail lowers herself on him once again, this time with uncoordinated movements.

"What do you think you're doing?" I hiss at Vlad. This wasn't what we'd discussed.

"I want to see if a corpse can ejaculate," he states in all seriousness.

"W . . . what?" Even to my ears, that sounds crazy.

But one glance at his face and I can see he's invested in this. Great! Another one of his science experiments.

I settle back in my chair, and we both watch as Abigail keeps on fucking herself on a dead man's cock. Time goes by, and nothing happens.

"Let's finish this and go." I get up to leave, already miffed with Vlad.

He doesn't seem to hear me, as he tilts his head to the right, his eyes focused on Abigail.

"Vlad!" I snap my fingers in front of him, but he just swipes my hand aside. He raises his eyes to look at me, a bored expression on his face.

"Fucking hell!" I curse, snatching my gun from his hand. "One thing I asked. Just one. And you had to ruin it."

"But how often do you get to see someone fuck a corpse?"hHe asks me, looking so innocent. I narrow my eyes at him.

"You're sick," I mutter under my breath. While I am not quite normal myself, I'm certainly nowhere near Vlad's level of fucked up. That is a competition I will always lose, as much as it pains me to admit.

Grabbing onto his jacket, I pull him to his feet, ready to end this. He seems to have other ideas, though, as he wraps his hand around my arm, pushing me out of the way.

My mouth drops open, my eyes wide as I look at him incredulously. Did he just push me? It's instinctive as my fist shoots out, nabbing his cheek. Head to the side, he checks his jaw for any damage, before slowly turning toward me, his eyes glinting with excitement.

"You want it rough, little goddess?" he says a second before he delivers an uppercut straight to my gut. I don't even get to wince in pain as I get ready to parry his next hit, all the while landing others of my own.

Fists flying, we're messing around at this point.

Then it all stops.

Vlad's got one hand wrapped around my throat, and with the other, he throws his dagger so it lodges straight in between Abigail's eyes as she was about to make her escape. Releasing me, he goes to check on both bodies.

I massage my neck, stretching a little.

"This is on you," I add when he turns his face at the blood pooling on the carpet. "We could have done it so much cleaner." I shake my head.

"If it wasn't for your brilliant idea to watch them fuck, maybe we wouldn't be here, would we?"

"Hey!" I exclaim, outraged.

"Let's call it a draw," he sighs. "You wanted to learn about sex and I . . . well, I wanted to learn about sex after death. I'd say we both got what we wanted."

"No, I did not." I cross my arms, pissed at how everything had turned out. "You ruined a perfectly good chance! How am I supposed to get good at it now?" The more I think about this failed attempt, the angrier I get.

Next time, I'm making sure Vlad is as far away as possible from me when I try anything similar.

"I don't know, practice? Should be like fighting. Practice makes best," he says with a shrug, setting about decapitating Bentham. We need to show proof that the man is dead.

"But I can't do that." I frown. He's right that practice makes best, but it wouldn't work for me in this scenario. "There's only one man I want, and I need to be the best at sex so I can blow his mind. Then he'll fall madly in love with me, and we'll live happily ever after." My soliloquy finished; I breathe out a dreamy smile.

"I don't know, B. Figure something out. Seduce him in disguise if you must, but stop compromising our missions. This isn't the first time you've been absent-minded because of that wimp."

For once, I overlook his insult as I latch onto his previous words. Seduce him in disguise? Get him to fuck me? My mind is slowly working, putting together all the variables, when suddenly a big smile stretches across my face.

"You're a genius!" I jump up and down in excitement. I dash to his side and give him a big kiss on the cheek. "That's exactly what I'll do!" Why didn't I think of this before? It's simply the best solution.

"This is you trying to make it up to me, isn't it?" I arch an eyebrow at Vlad as he's pretending to check out the wigs.

"Who? Me?" He feigns innocence, passing me a white-haired one. I put it on and then look in the mirror.

"It makes me look old," I scowl, turning my attention to the other colors.

"Might be in your favor. He might not be into the whole snatching the cradle thing you got going on."

"I'm not that young." I say, even though, objectively, I might be too young for him. But he doesn't need to know my age. I put the wig back and browse the other colors. I can't seem to decide what I want to go for.

Vlad passes me another one, and I'm about to refuse, given his obviously questionable tastes, when I notice the color.

Pink.

I snatch it out of his hands, putting it on immediately. A short, straight bob cut, the wig has a pink, almost magenta hue to it. The bangs end just above my eyebrows. As I study all the angles, I get another idea.

"I should get some contacts too." If my goal is to

eventually blow Theo's mind as myself, then I need to make myself as unrecognizable as possible.

Vlad grunts, already preoccupied with something else. I snicker at him and go to the checkout. It takes us a few hours of navigating different shops before my disguise is finally coming together.

"Don't you have someone else you can bring along? Like a girlfriend?" I hear Vlad mutter under his breath as I'm trying on a dress in the changing room.

"You know I don't." I pull aside the curtain to address him. "The last girlfriend I had decided to betray me after I pulled on her ponytails." Thinking of that incident has me fuming. I'd just wanted her hair tie — it was a pleasant color.

"And how long ago was that?" Vlad asks sarcastically, and I punch him.

"Shut it!" Yeah, it was during kindergarten, so what? I've had plenty of opportunities to make girlfriends, but it's too much effort. Why should I waste my time with another human being when there's only one person deserving of my full attention?

"That looks good," he suddenly mentions when he gets a better look at what I'm wearing. I'd chosen an incredibly short, skin-tight purple dress. "I've seen hookers wear that," he continues, and my face falls.

"Gee, thanks," I reply drily. Now I see why he's perpetually single — he simply has a way with compliments.

"Why? That's what you want, no? Hookers dress to attract." He shrugs.

I pause, digesting his words. He's not wrong. I may need to pull out the big guns, and by that I mean put all my assets on display.

"Fine. I'll take this." I pull the curtain deep in thought. I need to make this the perfect outfit to attract Theo's attention. Vlad is right in that regard. I need to make Theo salivate at the sight of me.

We spend the rest of the day going from shop to shop, buying more things until my outfit is done.

The last stop is at a beauty salon. Vlad checks out though, saying his duty is done. Seeing how restless he's become; I take pity on him and release him from best friend duty. I'm almost offended at his sigh of relief when he leaves, but then I remember he's not used to people, anyway. I must have worn him down.

Good!

The lady at the beauty salon is nice enough to explain what she's doing, and I pay careful attention so I can emulate the steps. I'd told her I wanted to become someone unrecognizable, and she'd complied.

Heavy contouring, highlight, bold eyeshadow and red lipstick. All that paired with the pink wig and the new green contacts will ensure I'm unrecognizable.

Now there's only one thing left to do — create the circumstances of our meetings.

For the past three years, I've been keeping tabs on

him, venturing out to see him now and then — the reality is just much sweeter than pictures. I know exactly what he's been up to, and who he's been meeting. And I'd made sure there were no women. I mean, not that hard in the first place, since he doesn't seem to have a particular interest in dating.

Which brings me to my current dilemma. I've put in so much effort to tempt him, but I still need an opportunity to work my charm on him.

I dial my go-to P.I. and I tell him to pay careful attention to where Theo goes.

One way or another, he's mine.

CHAPTER
Two

BIANCA

YOU COULD SAY I'm not the most patient person. Especially when it concerns Theo. That I've lasted so long is a testament to my sheer willpower and a realization that our meet-cute must be perfect.

It's been a few weeks now that I've been working on an approach to get to Theo with my new disguise. For a while, I'd thought it was hopeless. Maybe his lack of interest in dating coupled with my interference by eliminating all women from his proximity had made it impossible to approach him.

But then my P.I got back to me with an update. Theo's new position in the mayor's office meant he was spending a lot of time socializing with his peers at an exclusive club in the city — The Palace.

I'd done my research. The Palace wasn't just any club. It catered to the elite, and it provided both entertainment and . . . relief of a certain type. When I heard that, I was sure this was my moment.

It had taken me quite some time to infiltrate The Palace by becoming a server. You'd think it would be easy enough to score such a job, but I'd had to be vetted by three people (two of which I'd bribed) before I was officially hired. Like an excellent employee, I'd showed up every night for my shift, hoping to catch sight of Theo.

One week passed, then two weeks, and all I was getting was less sleep and more untoward remarks. The number of people I'd had to refrain from killing had been too high for my liking.

And so I find myself, once again, prancing around with a fake smile on my face, coked up from sniffing that damned powder, and ready to murder someone.

"Darlin' do me a favor and wipe this table down, will you?" an old man calls out to me. I have to grit my teeth at the appellation. I'm no one's darling, and I'd love to show Mr. Geezer at table two just how much I appreciate being cat-called. I've already suffered one attempted sexual assault for one night, and the only reason that man isn't dead is because I had to hurry inside and clock in. This job is too strict on working times.

I swallow a retort and start cleaning his table, trying to ignore the way he's leering at me, his gaze too focused on my cleavage.

Fucking hell!

I'm mentally debating whether or not I should shoot him when a group of people make their way inside and toward the VIP wing. I turn my head to study the newcomers and that's when I see him.

Theo.

My Theo.

He's here.

I strengthen my spine, my eyes following his movements as he heads toward the back of the club. Absent-mindedly, I drop the cleaning rag on the floor, my feet leading me toward one thing — him.

I quickly check with the girls working the VIP wing, and I resort to buying one of them out of her shift. Nevertheless, it's not long before I'm in the same space as him . . . so close I can practically smell him.

I close my eyes and inhale, a smile spreading on my lips. This is it. My chance.

Theo and his entourage settle down at one table and drinks are served. They seem to be deep in conversation, and as I see other girls walking around suggestively, I prepare myself.

This is it! I must make an impression.

So many times I've imagined this moment, and now that it's here, I don't even know what to do first.

Lap dance?

No, too common. There are already a few girls around doing that.

No, I have to make my entrance with a bang.

Determined to give my best, I school my features into a seductive smile, and I start walking.

Boobs out — check.

Hips swaying — check.

Biting my lips seductively — check.

And now . . eye contact — check.

His eyes flicker over my body and he doesn't look away. I advance slowly, and in the reddish light of the club, Theo looks even more attractive.

When I'm almost next to him, I notice his dilated pupils, the way his mouth is slightly agape.

How I wish I could kiss that mouth.

The way his eyes are roving over my body tells me he likes what he sees. I decide to be brazen, and as I hold his gaze, I slowly lower myself to my knees, placing one cheek on his thigh.

Some men are watching intently, while others are busy with their own entertainment.

But I tune it all out. I focus on the handsome man in front of me and I relish the proximity. This is the first time I've touched him in the flesh and I find my senses are getting numb, almost as if his mere touch is getting me drunk.

A shiver goes down my spine as I trace the contours of his muscles. Surprisingly, Theo is seriously packing. You would have never expected that behind his boring gray suits there would be a wall of muscle.

"You know the rules, handsome?" I turn to him, licking my lips suggestively. He's holding himself still, watching me intently.

"Look, but don't touch?" His voice is just like him — all male. There is a roughness to it that just serves to turn me on even more.

"This one, you can touch." I say, mesmerized by him. I keep touching him, my hand creeping higher and higher. I watch as his Adam's apple bobs up and down in anticipation.

"And what else?" He breathes out, almost as if he'd run a marathon. This might be my first attempt at seduction, but I can tell that I have him.

His hand comes up, his palm settling on my cheek. I lean into him, savoring the feel of his skin next to mine. His thumb slowly caresses my lips, smearing some red lipstick. I don't even think as I open my mouth and suck, my tongue gliding over his digit.

"You can do whatever you want to me." He has no idea just how much I mean those words.

My hands continue to roam over his thighs, going higher and reaching the growing bulge in his pants — the proof that he does, indeed, want me.

A little nervous, but mostly intoxicated by desire, I work on the zipper of his trousers. It might seem I'm going a little too slow, but I'm trying extremely hard to mask the sweat accumulating in my palms, and the fact that I have no idea what I'm doing.

I keep eye contact as I lower the fly and take him in hand. The moment I wrap my fingers around his cock, I let out a loud moan.

God, he's certainly not disappointing!

His clothes are definitely a camouflage for the man underneath, his generous size exciting and scaring me at the same time.

It might hurt.

I push that thought aside and I focus on the present.

Moving my hand up and down, I become more familiar with him. The warm flesh is beckoning, and I don't even think as I dip my head low and take him in my mouth. I lick the entire length before focusing on the head, sucking him, my tongue playing with the under-side — just as I'd seen the hooker do. Going by his reaction, I'm doing it well enough.

His head is thrown back, his mouth slightly parted, and his hooded eyes are watching me. Spurred by his expression, I take more of him inside, struggling to accommodate his size. I gag when the head hits the back of my throat, but he seems to enjoy this, so I will myself to relax.

Theo seems lost to sensation, his hands resting on top of my head and controlling my movements. The moment I slow down my ministrations, he takes over, lowering me over his length and fucking my mouth repeatedly. My eyes tear up as he holds me down, my lips at the base of his cock. His chest rumbles with a groan, and hot liquid shoots down my throat. I'm so fucking turned on right now, and the taste of him lingering on my tongue is making me grow even wetter. I'm two seconds away from grinding on his leg, so I lean back, still keeping my eyes on him. Now, I need to make a memorable exit.

Slowly, I lick my lips clean and give him a wink before standing up to leave.

His voice seems pained as he asks.

"Your name. What's your name?" My back is to him, so he doesn't see the slow tug of my lips, satisfaction settling deep into my core.

"Pink," I drawl, "my name is Pink." I don't look back as I head directly to the staff area.

My heart is beating loudly in my chest, my panties soaked. I did it. I fucking did it. And oh, was it everything I had thought it would be and more?

I prop myself against the lockers, trying to catch my breath, my mind slowly replaying every moment — every touch and every sound. God . . . My hand sneaks under the waistband of my panties, my fingers on my clit, seeking that relief. I turn my head to the side, stifling a moan as I bite into my shoulder. I hold on to the memory of his cock in my mouth, his cum on my tongue — a few strokes and I come, the orgasm so intense, I stagger off my feet.

Damn!

"Pink!" Someone yells from the door and reality crashes down on me, dissipating my previous high.

"Yes?" I respond, glad to see my voice sounds unaffected.

"The manager wants to see you." One girl peeks her head inside, looking at me with a scowl.

I nod and follow her.

I've had limited interactions with the manager, and of all the times he decides to call on me, he does it now? He should be grateful I don't have a gun attached to my thigh, or he'd . . .

"Pink." He stands up from his seat, his expression contrite. I almost roll my eyes, but I still need the job — especially now. He narrows his eyes at me before shaking his head.

"I've been made aware of what you just did," he starts, as if he can't watch the camera feed from behind his desk. There's CCTV all throughout the club. He probably jacks off to it, the pervert.

"Oh?" I raise my eyebrows, pretending to be oblivious to what he's referring to.

"You can't just perform sexual acts in the club. That's why we provide special rooms." He scowls at me.

"I'm so sorry," I say immediately, and I school my features to look guilty — and apologetic.

He looks me up and down for a second. I hope he won't get any ideas. I really don't want to kill him and lose my job.

"This is your first warning. Don't do it again. Next time, make them book a room." He waves his hand dismissively and I know I got off easy. Those rooms cost a fortune, so it's no wonder he doesn't want to lose potential clients.

I nod and quietly make my way out, heading back to the VIP wing and hoping Theo might still be there.

To my great disappointment, he's not.

Damn it!

Trudging my way to the club, I have to make a conscious effort to keep my eyes open. After last night, I'd barely slept a wink. Still, I have to be here on the off chance that Theo shows up. A quick glance at my watch and I realize I'm late.

Shit!

I increase my pace, hurrying to clock in before the absence is put on my record. Almost dashing through the club hallways, I greet the night manager and go to the lockers to change. As soon as I have my outfit on, I decide to head straight to the VIP lounge. If he's at the club, then he's most likely to be there.

The club is sectioned in two parts, one room for the regular people and another for the ones requiring more privacy. There is a dark tunnel connecting both of them, and only select people are allowed in — those with access to the entire club. Before I switch places with another girl working the VIP side, I have to be sure Theo is present. One night there and I'd realized that the girls were expected to be propositioned. I don't want to risk injuring anyone if I get pissed — especially someone important.

Being late also means there's less traffic in the tunnel at this time. I pause for a second to catch my breath and to compose myself. I still have to look my best.

I pat my dress down, making sure to emphasize the contour of my breasts. I'd seen the way Theo had looked at my cleavage, so I'd put on an extra-padded bra today. I'm trying to adjust one boob, when suddenly someone pulls on my arm.

I'm thrust against the wall, and my fight instincts kick in.

He didn't!

I feel a fiery breath on skin, skimming the curve of my neck and toward my ear.

"I've been looking for you, Barbie girl." His voice sends a shiver down my back, and I know instinctively who it is.

Theo!

"Is that so?" I ask breathlessly. The moment I confirm

his identity, my body does a one-eighty. Goosebumps cover my skin, and the increasing arousal I'm feeling has me crossing my legs to find some relief.

His hand moves up, trailing feather-like touches up my arm before dipping between my breasts. My breath hitches as he stops, and anticipation builds.

"We have unfinished business," he continues, his voice so suave — palpable sin. I don't trust myself anymore, and my hands grip onto his biceps for support.

Oh la la, more muscle.

"Do we?" God, I must sound like an idiot, but it's his fault. How can I be coherent when the object of my desire is within reach — close enough to touch?

"You're such a fucking tease," he rasps, his face moving closer, "you think you can strut into the room, blow me until I see stars and then simply disappear?"

"I thought men enjoyed the chase." His hand is moving down, tantalizingly close to the spot that needs him the most.

"Oh, I do. I spent hours last night imagining all the ways I'd fuck you when I caught you." A whimper escapes my lips, and I feel myself growing wetter by the second. "Tell me, Barbie girl," his lips are hovering right above my flesh, "how do you like to get fucked?" His tongue sneaks out to lick right below my ear. When I feel the warm contact on my neck, I sigh, closing my eyes. My whole body contracts, my fingers digging into his arms. His chuckle brings me down to earth. "One touch of my lips and you came," he says, amused. I'm breathing hard, trying to gather my wits.

"I see you, Barbie girl. You want it rough," his teeth nibble at my earlobe "hard and fast in a body-bruising way. You want me to fuck you like the dirty little girl you are." Theo skims his fingers up my thigh, tracing the material of my panties.

"Please," I moan, overwhelmed by the sensory overload.

"Please what, Barbie girl?"

"Please fuck me." I want to tell him how much I want him, how I might die if I don't feel him inside of me right this second, but words seem to fail me.

"Your wish is my command." I feel his smile against my neck, and in no time, he rips the fishnets off my body, pushing my panties to the side. His hand sneaks between my lips, and I almost die from the sensation.

"So wet," he murmurs, his tone dripping with satisfaction as he grazes over my clit, inserting one digit inside of me, "and so tight."

"Only for you." Only ever for you. He's the first and only man I'd allow to touch me like that.

"Is that so?" He removes his finger and I'm suddenly left bereft. I whimper at the loss, but watch as he brings it to his mouth, licking off my juices.

Fuck! I'm in trouble.

It all happens so fast I can barely register it. In one

swoop, he has me backed further into the wall, my legs wrapped around his waist. His hard length comes into contact with my center, and I let out a loud moan.

I need this like I need my next breath, and with shaky fingers I try to unbutton his pants.

"In a hurry, are we?" He breathes against my face. I can only nod, and his hands replace mine, taking his cock out and stroking it along the wet seam of my pussy.

"Fuck!" I cry out, knowing it's just a matter of seconds now.

He fumbles to put on a condom and before I know it, he's pushing against me.

"So fucking tight," he rasps in my ear, and I turn my head to the side, hoping he won't see the tears in my eyes.

It burns!

Shit! I should have expected the pain given his size.

His hands are on my ass, hauling me over his length until he's fully embedded inside of me. He groans low in his throat, his forehead resting on mine. I lock my legs behind his back, holding him to me, hoping the pain will subside.

"You're wrecking me, Barbie girl," he says before his mouth seeks mine. My first kiss, and it's not gentle or tentative. No, it's a full-on parrying of tongues and mashing of mouths. I revel in the sensation of having him inside of me, of finally becoming one.

Because he is mine. He just doesn't know it yet.

He pulls back, withdrawing almost all the way before thrusting in again. His tongue is emulating the movements of his cock and I no longer care about pain, or anything really. It's just us — me and him.

His fingers dig into my ass, his movements gaining momentum. He thrusts into me like a madman, the tip of his cock hitting deep inside and making me gasp.

"Goddamn it." His grunts are huskier and one hand travels up to my neck, grabbing me in a painful hold and twisting my head around so I'm looking straight into his eyes. "You're a witch, Pink. You've bewitched me," he murmurs before kissing me harder. His mouth trails down my neck until he reaches my tits. Tugging my dress down, he pops one nipple into his mouth, suckling.

God!

His teeth scrape my breasts as he licks and laps at me. Just as he moves to the other breast, my hands find their way into his hair, urging him on, drawing him closer.

Theo picks up speed, his cock moving in and out of me before he suddenly stills, his entire body taut with tension.

"Witch," he whispers again as he comes. I wrap my arms around him, holding onto him as he rides his pleasure.

Breathing hard, he raises his head from the crook of my neck, his forehead full of perspiration.

"Shit!" he curses. "You didn't come, did you?" My first intention is to lie and say that I did, so I open my mouth to do that, but the words get stuck into my throat as his fingers deftly work my clit. He's still inside of me, and that fullness coupled with the tingles from my clit has me coming in no time.

"Good," he praises, "good girl."

My lips stretch into a smile as he helps me down, withdrawing from me completely. One glance down has me panicking though, as I spot some blood at the base of the condom.

I immediately get on my knees, quickly removing the rubber and taking his length in my mouth.

"Just like that." His hand comes over my hair, brushing it aside. "Clean that cock real nice, my dirty little girl."

And I do. Because that's all I ever want to be.

His dirty little girl.

CHAPTER
Three

THEO

"HER BODY HAD BRUISES EVERYWHERE, and the forensic pathologist suggested she was likely beaten to death."

I nod, my fingers playing absentmindedly with a pencil. This debriefing is taking longer than I expected, considering I know all the information presented.

The mayor had personally sent me to oversee this case within the NYPD, since the murder was that of a high-profile individual. Even knowing what's at stake, my mind simply can't focus on what's being said.

All I can think of is Pink.

The way she'd come for me. The noises she'd made when I'd fucked her tight little pussy. I almost groan out loud at the memory of her clenching around my cock, her fingers pulling at my hair as I'd sucked a nipple in my mouth. The way I know for sure I'm returning for more.

I shift a little, feeling the blood rushing down to my lower region the more I picture her.

I'd forgotten what it was like to be with a woman. Hell, I don't even remember the last time I was with one. Years? More? After a couple of failed attempts as a teenager, I hadn't bothered anymore. Even those times had been more like a rite of passage, since the entire experience had been purely transactional.

But Pink . . . no one's ever gotten my attention like Pink did. Yes, this might be transactional too, but the attraction between us is palpable, pulsating in the air. Just being in the same room as her makes my senses prickle with awareness. She exudes such raw sexuality that I want to consume her whole. And I will.

"Mr. Hastings is here as a liaison to the mayor's office." The presenter's words wake me from my reverie, and I quickly close my eyes and take a deep breath. "Why don't you introduce yourself, Mr. Hastings?"

I stand up, putting on my best professional expression.

"Thank you," I say before continuing. "I am Theodore Hastings. I graduated from Quantico some years ago, but I've been off field work for a year now." I give some background information about my credentials before I launch into the importance of the case at hand.

"Romina Lastra, nee Agosti, isn't just any murder victim. Unofficially, her father, Rocco Agosti, is part of the Italian mafia. Our sources have identified several illegal businesses related to the Agosti name. Her husband is touted to be a mobster as well, but we haven't had many reports linking Valentino Lastra to any illegal activity." I take a deep breath. "It's all unofficial, of course, but we're talking about faction disputes here. And since right now the most probable culprit is her husband . . ." I let the words hang, and they seem to catch my meaning.

"We need to be careful in our investigation," one man notes, and I nod.

"Yes. The last thing we want now is to involuntarily cause a mob war. Knowing what's at stake, I want everyone to focus on this investigation." I turn to address the forensic team. "I'm not saying this to create any bias, rather I want you all to carefully examine the evidence and make sure you are as thorough as possible."

I go through a few more details before dismissing the meeting. When everyone's left the room, I take out my phone and see a few missed calls from Marcel. Worried it might be something urgent, I dial his number right away.

I'd met Marcel a couple of years ago by chance. We used to live in the same apartment building and I would often see him at the gym. He always kept to himself, and I'd noticed him shutting down every single attempt at flirtation with the opposite sex.

This one time, a girl had intruded too far into his personal space and touched him. I don't know exactly what had happened in that moment, but it was like watching someone flip a switch. Marcel had collapsed on the floor, his eyes wide and unblinking. He'd been unresponsive, so I'd immediately called an ambulance, going with him to the hospital.

He'd had a panic attack.

That day I'd learned of his aversion to touch and that it seemed to be directly connected to some trauma. I'd never pried, however, seeing how private of a person he was. But from our initial conversation at the hospital, where he'd thanked me for my involvement, a comfortable friendship had arisen.

The first year, we'd interacted mostly as neighbors, but slowly he'd become a little more comfortable talking to me.

"Marcel?" I ask when he answers the phone. "Is there something wrong?" Given his taciturn and aloof nature, it's exceedingly rare for him to be the one to initiate a call — let alone more.

"No." He pauses. "I was driving by the station and wanted to see if you're done with your meeting."

"Just finished."

"Great. I'm in the parking lot," he says, and he hangs up. Odd.

After I gather all my materials, I make my way to his car, getting in the passenger's seat.

"Kind of you to drop by," I add drily after I fasten my seat belt.

"I was in the area." He shrugs. Starting the car, he drives toward our apartment building. "How was the meeting? Any updates on the perpetrator?" He asks, quite possibly the most words he's ever said at once.

"Not really. The husband's still the primary suspect, although I want to revisit the evidence," I say almost absentmindedly.

"Do you even have other suspects?"

I turn to look at him. His expression is somber, his eyes on the road.

"You know I can't say that," I add jokingly, a little curious about his sudden interest in the case.

"Right," Marcel says, although his tone doesn't seem too convincing.

"Are you done with finals?" I change the subject. He's in his first year of law school, even though I can't imagine how that works for him, with his anti-social tendencies.

"Yeah." That's all he says, and shaking my head, I drop it. I know I'm not likely to get more from him.

We get to the apartment building and we each go our separate ways.

The moment I open the door, I am assaulted by my

little roommates, all crowding at my feet and meowing loudly.

"There, there, did you miss me that much?" Dropping my briefcase, I stoop down to take them into my arms. It's not that easy to juggle four cats in my arms, but our daily routine is already established, so they know not to squirm.

I take them with me to the couch, and I make sure to equally pet each one. One shelter I volunteer at seems to always have too many cats and too little funds. Somehow, I always end up adopting the cats that have nowhere to go. I'd told myself I would stop, especially since they are awfully competitive about my attention and can get quite mean. But last time, when I'd seen an injured white kitten on the verge of being booted, I couldn't find it in me to say no — especially since it reminded me of my childhood cat, Spot.

Taking out some cat food, I lay it on the floor and watch, amused as they fight over who eats first.

Thinking of taking a shower, I head to the bathroom. Seeing the house so empty, so bare, I'm struck by how bleak my life is. What do I even do? I wake up, go to work, then back home and sleep again. It's all a never-ending cycle, a self-imposed routine that I'd drilled into my skull for years now. Maybe my encounter with Pink did more than awaken my dead libido. Maybe I'm finally allowing myself to consider what it would be like to have a warm body to wake up to in the morning, someone to share happiness and concerns.

Not for the first time, I have to wonder what I'm doing with my life. Is it even worth it? This revenge I set out to deliver more than a decade ago?

What will happen when I'm done? The wind will still howl through the hallway and the rooms will still be empty.

I have to admit there is a side of me that yearns for a partnership, for family and for kids . . . but there's also the other side of me that vowed to see justice made. And somehow, they don't seem to be mutually compatible.

I can't ever, in good faith, invite danger into my home, knowingly put my wife and kids at risk.

The following day, I head to the mayor's office for a short meeting on Romina's case. I'm ushered inside by his secretary, but I'm surprised to see he is not alone. Martin Ashby, renowned billionaire and the financial force behind the mayor, casually turns to me.

"Hastings, long time no see," he exclaims, rising to

his feet to shake my hand. I'd run into Martin quite a few times since working with the mayor. You could say he knows everyone who is anyone in the city, and I get the feeling a lot of them owe him favors.

I don't exactly know how the mayor and Martin met, or the extent of their relationship, but it is unusual to see them together in his office. Such meetings are better relegated for more private quarters.

"Mr. Ashby." I incline my head. He motions me to the settee and the mayor hands me a drink.

"I was just asking Justin to join me on the golf course this weekend. Why don't you come too?" Martin adds, nodding toward the mayor.

"If I am free." I attempt a smile. Golf is boring. Golf with these people would be even more boring.

"Come on, Hastings. It's a miracle I bumped into you. It's been what . . . a year? Yeah, one or two years since I saw you last. Don't tell me you're purposefully avoiding me." His tone is joking, but I can see the underlying threat. Martin enjoys keeping tabs on everyone, and that seems to include me too.

"I'll make an effort," I amend, hoping this answer is better.

"You should drop by my house sometime, meet my daughter. You're single, right?" he continues and I maintain my expression.

"Indeed," I answer, gritting my teeth. I don't like where this is going.

"Marvelous. I think you'd like my daughter. Meek little thing, and very sheltered. She'd make the perfect housewife." He praises her attributes, and I have to stifle the urge to roll my eyes. Has anyone told him we're not in the fifties anymore?

"Yes," he continues, looking me up and down. "I think you two would suit just nice."

"And how old is your daughter?" I try to shift the conversation a little, not wanting him to proclaim me his son-in-law in the next second.

He pauses, narrowing his eyes as if trying to remember. "She just turned nineteen. Ripe for the plucking." He raises an eyebrow at me suggestively and I nearly gag. Nineteen? That's way too young for me — there's almost a decade standing between us.

I force a smile and try to steer the conversation in a different direction. The last thing I want is for Martin to offer me his barely legal daughter. But then, looking at his sleazy ass, I guess it's to be expected he'd try to pimp out his own child. I suddenly feel sorry for the girl and for whatever awaits her.

CHAPTER
Four

BIANCA

SUCKING MY CHEEKS IN, I apply more contour, wanting my cheekbones to be more defined — and my age hidden. Pouting, I angle my face in the mirror so I can check if it's blended well. When I'm finally satisfied, I put on red lipstick and it's done. I hurry outside and hail a cab toward The Palace.

Hard to believe it's been almost a year since I first saw Theo at the club. That time in which I met with Theo weekly, sometimes even more often. I've gotten so used to having him close that the thought of it ending terrifies me.

No! Never!

Who am I kidding? I'm becoming greedier. Once a week is no longer enough. Just like my coke addiction got out of control, so did my yearning for him. I want him with a passion so strong, I'd kill anyone who dared interfere. I long for him and even sleep eludes me when he's not around — ok, maybe the coke has something to do with that too. That doesn't change the fact that I need more.

I want to own him.

As soon as I am at the club, I head directly to our usual room, hoping I'll be early enough to compose myself and look the embodiment of cool chic. I punch in the code, and I'm extremely surprised to see him already inside. I take a deep breath and I put on my most seductive smile.

"Theo?" I purr, my voice an octave lower than normal. He half-turns, his eyes eating me up. He casually makes his way toward me, grasping my chin between his thumbs.

"Now, what did we agree on, Barbie girl?" His eyes are fixed on my mouth, and I immediately know what he wants.

In no time, I take off my cardigan to reveal the lace lingerie I'd worn just for him. Then I drop to my knees.

"Sir." I bat my lashes at him, and he regales me with a smirk. There's something different about him today, some type of coiling tension. His thumb swipes across my mouth, smearing the red lipstick.

"You have quite a mouth on you, dirty girl. Why don't you put it to better use?" I tilt my head, looking at him with feigned innocence. It only spurs him further as he unzips himself, thrusting his cock in my mouth. I quickly accommodate him, sucking and lapping at him like I'd learned in the past year.

"Enough," he commands, and I immediately obey. "On the table. Ass in the air."

The lingerie I'd worn comprises a bralette that reaches my midriff and a thong that connects with a garter. Knowing how good my body looks in it, I give him a spectacle as I crawl on all fours toward the table, wiggling my ass in the air the entire time. I prop myself on the table and look back slightly. His eyes are watching me intently, and a shiver goes down my back.

Whenever we are in the same room, there's this sizzling electricity in the air, and even the hair on my arms stands up. But when he looks at me like that . . . like he wants to eat me alive, I feel like combusting from a mix of desire and arousal — and if it goes unfulfilled for much longer, I will.

He comes behind me, securing a blindfold over my eyes. His fingers trail down my spine and toward my butt. When he reaches my thong, he slowly slips it off my legs, leaving me bare for his view.

"Sir?" I ask when nothing happens. Then, suddenly, his mouth is on my pussy. I gasp as I feel his tongue probing deeper, stroking me inside. My entire body shudders, and I grip the edge of the table to hold myself still.

"You like that, don't you?" He breathes against me,

the warm air of his breath mixing with my wetness and making me squirm.

"Please, sir," I say, wanting him to put me out of my misery. Two fingers join his mouth, and he works them in and out of me while his mouth is on my clit, sucking and nibbling. I clench around his digits, the orgasm hitting me so hard I see black before my eyes. Flat on the table, I almost pass out from the intensity of the pleasure.

Theo rises, his hands once again on my butt and massaging my cheeks. Taking some wetness from my pussy, he spreads it higher, towards my other hole.

"Tell me, Barbie girl, have you ever been fucked here?" he asks, the tip of his finger pushing in ever so slightly. My breath hitches, and excitement builds anew.

"No," I whisper, barely able to let out a sound.

"What was that my dirty little girl? I didn't hear you." His fingers go even deeper before retreating.

"No, never," I say with more conviction.

"And you'll let me be the first?" he asks, still playing with me. He might not know it, but he has all my firsts.

"Will I be your first too?" I don't know what prompts me to voice this, especially since I know he doesn't like it when I speak back to him in the bedroom. The moment the question is out of my mouth, though, I take a deep breath, awaiting my punishment.

A deep chuckle permeates the air.

"Would you like that, Barbie girl? Would you like to be my first?"

"Yes." I don't even think as I say this. The thought of Theo touching someone else physically pains me.

He doesn't answer. Instead, his palm comes down on my ass, the slap loud, the pain making me flinch.

"You know why I'm doing this, don't you?" he asks just as he slaps my ass again.

"Yes, sir," I meekly respond.

"Good." He hums his approval, continuing to dole out the punishment. Slap after slap, my ass must be red by now. I almost tear up from the pain, but I've had worse, so I steel myself.

Then he stops.

"You are, Barbie girl. You're the first," he says, amused. "Does that please you?"

"Yes. Yes, sir." My tone is entirely too enthusiastic as I reply.

"Enough that you'll let me fuck your ass?" His hand comes down on the battered cheeks again, but this time he's tenderly caressing them.

"Yes."

He leaves my side for a second, before returning and pouring some type of oil on my back. He spreads it around and massages it into my skin. Going lower, he pours even more liquid between my ass cheeks. His finger moves in and out of my hole, lathering the entire area with the lubricant.

I'm only getting used to the unfamiliar sensation when his finger is replaced by the head of his cock. He pushes in slowly, the pressure almost too much. I hold on to the table as he inches his way inside of me. After the initial burn, the pain gives way to a pleasant fullness. I wiggle my butt around, and his cock slips inside even more.

"That's it, Barbie girl. If you could see the way your ass is eating up my cock," he grunts, his breathing irregular.

"More. Please, sir." At my words, Theo grips my hips and pushes all the way inside, the feeling of him there so abundant, I can't help but release a whimper. He's balls-deep in my ass, and the thought of it feels me with giddiness.

And I'm his first.

"Oh," I moan as he retreats, only to surge forward once more.

Mine. Yes, he's mine.

At first, his thrusts are slow and tentative, but once he sees he's not hurting me in any way, he increases his speed.

And oh, God!

The pressure gives way to pleasure, and my entire body is tingling with the nearing of an orgasm.

Just as I'm about to reach that height, he pulls out, flipping me on my back and removing the blindfold. In no time, his cock is back in my ass, his hands on my tits.

"That's it, Barbie girl. I want you to see who's fucking you," he rasps as he increases the speed of his thrusts, his fingers playing with my puckered nipples.

The combined sensations are too much, and my mouth forms a silent 'o' as I keep myself from screaming out.

One hand still on my breast, the other moves lower and he circles my clit at the perfect time. Overwhelmed by the intensity of the orgasm, my eyes roll in the back of my head, my body convulsing and tightening over his cock.

"Fuck yeah," Theo grunts, pulling out and discarding the condom on the floor before taking himself in hand and coming all over my stomach. "Damn it, Pink, a man needs health insurance with you." He gives me a lopsided smile before collapsing next to me on the table.

"Health insurance or a body bag?" I ask before I can think it through.

Great with the morbid humor, B!

Theo doesn't reply for a second before bursting into laughter.

"You're one of a kind, Barbie girl."

Once back in the cab, I pull at my wig, my frustration increasing by the moment. It always happens when I have to leave Theo, knowing full-well I'd like nothing more than to attach myself to his hip.

Before I head home, I do a quick detour to my spare apartment to shed my disguise and make sure I look presentable. Even though I always do my best to avoid my father, it's best to not raise suspicions — not that he'd think I'm capable of such increased mental capacity, me being a woman and all that.

When I finally reach home, I tiptoe around the grand hall, aiming to head directly to my room. To my great dismay — and annoyance — my father is at home.

"Bianca," he calls my name as he struts in, his face sporting a perpetual scowl.

I square my shoulders and look down.

"Yes?" My voice is soft and submissive.

"Andrew told me you won't be home this weekend. What's that about?" He narrows his eyes at me, and I curse Drew for a moment.

"I have a competition for college." I keep my explanation short, knowing he doesn't really care. He scoffs at my words, not because I'm going to the competition, but because he's still pissed at me for attending college.

"Don't do anything to embarrass me." He stops next to me, and I make myself look meeker.

"Of course, Father."

"Good," he huffs out, leaving.

I take a deep breath, thankful the meeting went well. All my plans are contingent on keeping both my identities separate.

The following day, I leave early, heading straight to Penn Station to take the train. It takes an hour and a half to get to Philadelphia, where I'm supposed to meet with Vlad at the Rittenhouse Hotel. Before leaving the station, though, I go to a restroom and change my clothes, donning my Artemis disguise — leather pants, a leather jacket on top of a black shirt, and a long red wig. I holster two guns in the waistband of the pants and hide two daggers in my boots. With everything in place, I put on a pair of sunglasses and swing the backpack on, exiting the station.

The hotel is a short walk from the station, so I swiftly check in under an assumed name and head to the room. Not surprisingly, Vlad isn't here yet.

I do a quick scan about the room, familiarizing myself with the layout. Like many others, this mission involves some fake seduction on my part, luring the victim to the room, and then doing the killing. Whenever we have such missions, Vlad takes the role of coordinator while I become the bait. I roll my eyes at the designations, although I have to begrudgingly admit that he is the brains behind our missions. Alas, at least I get the kill.

It's proven to be a point of contention many times — who gets the kill? We have many games we play to establish who will be the one to pull the trigger, or in his case, the knife. We're both incredibly competitive people so the games can become . . . intense.

My phone rings and I see a text from Vlad. He's running late.

Cursing under my breath, I decide to head to the bar for some refreshments. I have enough time until our victim, a business executive, is set to arrive at the hotel. Before I leave the room, I take out a key and open the small locket I carry around my neck; I sprinkle a little white powder on it. I bring the tip of the key to my nose and inhale, needing my daily dose of energy. Making sure there's no white residue, I leave the room.

I'm in the hallway, waiting for the elevator when I hear some disturbance. I tip my glasses lower on my nose, trying to see who's causing the commotion.

A burly man in his thirties is dragging a girl around by her hair, all the while cursing her out. Her features are drawn in pain, and she seems resigned to whatever he has in store for her.

They move to pass by me, and maybe it's my boredom, but I put my foot forward to trip the man. He sees it just in time, though, and stops.

"What the fuck, bitch?" He shifts toward me, and the girl yelps in pain.

"Didn't your mother teach you how to treat a lady?" I raise an eyebrow at him, my eyes moving over the girl's figure and noting the various bruises.

He throws his head back and laughs. At this point, I grow annoyed, so I just wait for him to dig his grave even more.

"Lady? This?" He smirks arrogantly and shoves the girl to the floor. He turns his attention to me, looking me up and down. "You don't look like a lady to me, either." He drawls and I have to roll my eyes.

"Really?" I ask drily, begging him to make a move.

"Right, you're one of those biker chicks, aren't you? The ones that like it rough." His smile grows as he lifts one hand to touch me. It doesn't get that far. I catch his hand mid-air, and I bend it at an odd angle, hearing a couple bones break.

He yelps in pain, and a smile tugs at my lips at the sound, not unlike the one the girl made.

"What the fuck!" He tries to jab me with the other arm, so I lift my foot and I kick him in the chest — hard. He falls down next to the girl. I'm about to give him some more of his own medicine when the girl covers him with her body.

"Leave him alone!" she cries, and I stop, flabbergasted.

"You . . . You're defending him?" I ask, almost in disbelief.

"He's my husband," she replies, cooing all over the motherfucker's body.

"Who beats you."

"You don't know anything!" she says accusatorily,

helping him to his feet and moving out of reach. He's shooting daggers at me, but I guess he's not much of a tough guy now with a broken wrist.

I let this one slide, since the girl's chosen her own fate. She could have asked, and I would have gladly killed him for her.

I shrug, putting it out of my mind. Her loss.

The elevator doors open, and I go to the ground floor. I plop myself at the bar and order a dirty martini.

One drink shouldn't be too bad, right?

I sip the drink slowly, when I see a group of people come in. All are dressed in formal suits, and given that it's still noon, I'm a little intrigued.

Is my businessman early?

I shift a little so I can have a full view of the new arrivals. It's . . . five people. No, I count six. And one of them is . . . my eyes widen and I quickly push my glasses up my nose.

Theo!

What is he doing here? I lower my head, keeping my focus on my drink. He wouldn't recognize me, I'm certain of it. Vlad's told me that unless you're specifically looking for them, the similarities aren't that glaring. Especially since I'm not wearing any makeup right now, and I have long red hair.

As I try to convince myself that he won't recognize me, I can't help it as I sneak a few glances toward his entourage. They just sat down on the couches in the dining area, still within my field of vision.

Half an hour later, and another martini down, I'm still staring. God, he is handsome! Especially there, in his element, looking all cocky and self-assured. I almost get wet just thinking about those big hands of his on my body, him pounding into me.

A sigh escapes me, and the bartender regards me a little suspiciously.

"Another one," I say, pointing to my drink.

"But . . ." He looks as if he might argue, but shaking his head, he prepares me another martini.

I bring the glass to my lips just as Theo and the men with him stand up, shaking hands. It's at that moment that a loud noise permeates the air.

My semi-dulled senses are suddenly on alert, looking toward the direction of the noise.

Shots.

I hop off the chair, my focus on Theo and him alone. Everyone is panicking, some people falling to the floor. The entrance doors open wide to show at least four heavily armed men coming inside.

Fuck!

I spare a glance at Theo and the position of his body tells me he's about to do something stupid. In a few steps I'm on him, tackling him to the ground.

"Stay still," I hiss, trying to mask my voice. He frowns at me, but nods.

"I see four," he remarks.

"Five," I whisper, noting another one in the back.

I take out the guns from the waistline of my pants, and I hand him one. He should know how to use one, given his background.

He eyes the weapon suspiciously before taking it. The men with him are all on the floor, shriveled up with fear. For a second, I'm curious what the meeting was all about, but seeing that we have more pressing matters at hand, I decide to look into that later.

"You take those, I'll take the ones on the right." I point in two directions, and he nods.

Pointing my gun toward the armed men, I shoot.

Maybe I drank too much.

It takes me twice as many shots to kill the man, mostly because my eyesight is a little fuzzy.

Fuck!

I blink twice, trying to get a hold of myself, when a bullet whizzes past me and embeds itself in the man aiming at me. I turn slightly to see Theo give me a small signal to keep my head in the game. If this weren't such a life and death situation, I would have swooned. My Theo just saved me.

I stifle the smile making its way on my face, and I straighten myself.

"How many more?" I ask, my back hitting his as we scour for the other men.

"I got two," he says.

"Same. So, one?" He shakes his head slightly.

"I think so."

People are still on the ground, shaking, and Theo tries his best to assure them they're in safe hands and that he is police.

We move around, guns pointed, backs glued to each other. Then another man opens fire. I see him just in time to push Theo out of the way and shoot. The bullet finds its way between his eyes and he drops dead.

"Nice," Theo praises.

We scout the area anew, and no other gunmen are present. I realize I need to make myself scarce. I take the stairs a few floors up before taking the elevator to the top where my room is.

To my surprise, Vlad is already there. I frown. When did he arrive?

"Did you enjoy your little break?" he asks drily, flinging a new set of clothes in my direction, together with a blonde wig. "You were reckless. Again." He rolls his eyes at me and comes closer, sniffing me. "And drunk."

"I only had a couple," I add.

"A couple too many when we had a mission." He shakes his head. "You don't have to worry about that, at least. I took care of it."

"What do you mean? Did you steal my kill?" I'm incensed, and my fingers tighten over my gun.

"Didn't you have two of those?" he asks in that bored manner of his. My eyes widen. Shit!

"They're untraceable," I respond, but he's not having it.

"Doesn't matter. Reckless. I should kill that suit of yours one of these days, maybe then your productivity will increase."

"Don't you dare!" I burst out, my voice louder than I'd intended. "Never threaten Theo again, or you'll have an enemy out of me."

"Another one?" He snorts. "Bring it on, *malyshka*. I wonder, between the two of us, who would win? I'll even let you sober up," he adds, amused.

"Sure," I answer sarcastically, taking the clothes and heading to the bathroom.

Thing is, I don't know who would win. Unless he loses his mind, my bet would be on Vlad, not that I'd ever tell him that.

Mission accomplished by Vlad, I get to return home early. We'd slipped out of the hotel while the police were investigating the area, barely escaping the scrutiny, since Theo was apparently seeking a red-head with sick aim. I smile to myself, satisfied that even in my disguise, I'd managed to show Theo my abilities, and we'd even fought side by side.

I sigh just thinking about it. How it would feel to be myself with Theo, for us to be a team — us against the world. The sad thing is that I know that will never happen. Knowing his obsession with justice, I'm well-aware he would never accept a vigilante like me. Hell, who am I even kidding, a killer like me?

I'm lost in my thoughts when my father once again calls out to me. What is it with him these days? Usually, we interact every other week.

"Bianca." He purses his lips, looking down at me. I really want to roll my eyes at him, but instead I just stretch my lips in a sweet smile.

"Yes, Father?"

"We're having important guests next Sunday. Be sure to be present and on your best behavior."

"Of course, Father," I agree immediately, although inside I'm fuming at his audacity to order me around. If only I had a knife right now, I'd stab and stab, and for once, I'd enjoy the blood messily spurting around.

"Good. Dress conservatively. These are important men, and they don't . . ." He looks at me as if I disgust him, "like when women are too forward. Make sure you know your place." He turns on his feet and leaves.

If looks could kill, he'd be on the floor right now. They don't like women who are too forward? My lip curls in disdain. Fucking pussies. They're just afraid to be put in their place by a woman.

Oh, how sweet it would be to make them eat their words and show them exactly what a woman can do. I guess I am a hypocrite though, since I'm holding so hard onto my meek girl image just so I can one day appeal to Theo.

CHAPTER
Five

THEO

"YOU'RE sure he was the target?" Putting the phone on speaker, I head to the mirror to arrange my tie.

"Yeah. We found detailed plans at their hideout. They'd been following him for a while." My friend from the Philly force recounts how they'd ransacked the place and what they'd found.

"At least you can close the case," I add drily.

"True. Thanks for the effort. If it weren't for you and that woman, more people would have gotten hurt."

I grunt something and hang up.

No one had been able to identify the mysterious woman from the scene of the shooting. Even her gun was untraceable — black market. But she'd been one hell of a markswoman, even drunk. A smile tugs at the corner of my lips as I remember smelling the alcohol on her breath.

The police had concluded that the target had been an electronics company CEO. He'd recently laid off half of his workforce due to some financial difficulties, but the workers were under the impression that it was a case of embezzlement and poor management rather than just a poor turnover. While the shooters are dead now, the investigators found enough evidence to prove that it was indeed a case of syphoning funds and the CEO is now under arrest and pending trial.

I spare a glance at the clock on the wall and sigh in relief. I still have time.

After being hounded by Martin one too many times, I'd finally accepted his lunch invitation. From what I'd gathered from the mayor, Martin likes to host monthly Sunday lunches with different influential men.

The only reason I'm looking forward to this event is because Martin's connections might help me advance my own plans.

As soon as I reach his house, I am greeted by a footman who leads me to the drawing room — very old-fashioned. Then again, Martin's entire persona is the epitome of old money, and his imposing mansion is just what you'd expect of him.

"You are a little early, Mr. Hastings," the footman comments. "The other guests have not yet arrived, and Mr. Ashby is still busy. He has instructed me, however, to show you to the drawing room, where his daughter will keep you company."

I struggle to keep a straight face at his words, mostly because I can recognize this for the ploy it is. Martin's daughter must be what, twenty by now? It's not as if he hasn't tried to orchestrate an introduction before. It seems it's finally worked out for him.

"Thank you," I reply with a tight smile.

As we walk toward the room, a sweet piano melody resounds in the house. The footman shows me to the door and takes his leave.

A little curious, yet mostly apprehensive, I push through the double doors and enter the room. Inundated by light, the room has ceiling-high windows that face the back of the house, the green lawn stretching into a forest in the distance. I follow the rays of the sun as they bathe a white piano that is situated in the middle of the room.

A girl, no, a woman, is seated at the piano, eyes closed, her hands gliding over the keys and emitting the most melodious sound I'd ever heard. I don't think she hears me come in. There's a tranquility to her face, the way it subtly moves to the tune of the song, the small, almost imperceptible movement of her eyes under her closed eyelids.

I stop, and I stare, transfixed.

Her black hair is long, the ends curling inward. It flows down her back almost like an ebony cascade. She's wearing an off-white gown that cups her breasts in a modest fashion before cinching at the waist and flowing downwards. With her pale skin, she almost looks like Snow White.

I shake myself, a little amused by the direction of my thoughts. I'd never thought myself particularly poetic, but the sight of this woman, so immersed in her music as if she's living in her own world, makes me wonder if she's even real. Makes me want to insinuate myself into her world.

I stand there, just watching, for what seems like an eternity. It's only a soft gasp, followed by an "Oh!" that has me alert again. Her eyes snap open and they focus on me. A deep black, I feel myself falling even more.

She might just be the most exquisite woman I've ever seen in my life, her natural beauty so pure and untouched.

"I didn't know there was someone in the room. My apologies." Her voice is just as melodious as the piano music.

"No, I should be the one to apologize. Your music is beautiful." She lowers her eyes slightly, a blush staining her cheeks.

"Thank you," she murmurs, raising up from the piano and coming to stand in front of me.

"You must be one of my father's guests, no?" She gazes up at me, her eyes wide and innocent. She's tiny, her head barely reaching the middle of my chest. Her height, coupled with her slender frame, serves as a friendly reminder that she's almost a decade younger than me — clearly off limits.

"Theodore Hastings," I introduce myself, holding out my hand to her. She gives me a timid smile, hesitantly putting her hand in mine.

"Bianca Ashby."

The contact is brief, but it's enough to mess with my head. She probably has no idea what she does to me, the way my eyes follow the curve of her neck, the swell of her breasts as she invites me to sit down.

I swallow hard, and I try to think of the most disgusting crime scenes I've ever witnessed, hoping the gore will put a damper on my growing erection.

Bianca smiles sweetly at me, but she doesn't attempt to continue the conversation, too shy to even look me directly in the eye.

"Your father told me you're in college?" I try to remember anything Martin might have mentioned about her.

She gives me a soft nod.

"And what are you studying?" God, once again, I feel entirely too old for her.

"Social Studies."

"Really? Why?" I wouldn't have expected that answer from a rich girl. But then, she doesn't look like the typical spoiled little rich girl.

"I want to help people," she says, lowering her gaze as if she's ashamed of her dreams. "I want to make a difference for those less fortunate than me. I know I'm in a position of power and privilege because of my father, so I want to do something to give back to society," she finishes saying this, and I can't help but look at her in awe. She can't be real, can she?

So gorgeous and poised, and she has a big heart too? I swallow hard, the need to touch her is too overwhelming, but I control myself.

"That's a commendable aspiration," I praise, and I'm regaled by one of those beautiful smiles of hers.

Fuck! I'm in trouble.

We don't get to talk much further, as Martin strides in with a few other men. After some brief introductions, we are all ushered to the dining room.

By some luck of fate, Bianca is seated in front of me, so I continue to study her, her beauty something I've never encountered before. And it's not just her looks. There is something about her that pulls me and draws me in.

The conversation flows, and I notice that Bianca continues to smile, but doesn't say much else. Granted, no one seems to address her directly. Even Martin seems to forget the fact that his daughter is sitting at the table, his stories becoming bawdier and teetering on the vulgar side. Bianca maintains her gentle smile, even though I can tell there's a certain tightness to it.

I catch her eye and I give her a reassuring nod,

hoping it would comfort her to know she is not forgotten. She blushes and looks down at her plate.

"What about your daughter? She's of age, isn't she?" One of the older men, Anthony Bering, leers at her.

"That she is," Martin smirks.

"Tell me girl, do you have a boyfriend?" He turns his attention wholly on her, and Bianca shifts a little, clearly uncomfortable.

"She's not allowed to," Martin comments, taking a sip of his wine.

"Let her answer. Why isn't she talking?" Bianca lowers her gaze even more.

"I taught her well, Bering, she knows when to shut up," her father interjects, pride reflected in his gaze.

"She's a meek little thing, isn't she? Perfect for plucking. Probably a virgin too." He can't seem to stop talking, and looking at Martin, he has no intention of putting a stop to this. Bianca's cheeks are burning, and she is trying awfully hard to ignore the comments.

"That's not a way to talk to a lady," I interject, sick of this bawdy talk, especially in Bianca's presence.

"Lady? Tell me, Ashby, how much do you want for her?" Bering chuckles.

"How much are you willing to pay?" Martin raises an eyebrow and I feel my anger rising. Surely, it's just a joke, as much as it is in poor taste.

"I don't know," Bering continues, his eyes roving over Bianca's form. "I don't think she knows how to please a man. Do you, little bird?" He stands up, his fingers on her chin and raising her head up.

Seeing his pudgy little hands on her, I don't even think, I just react. In a matter of seconds, I have him by the collar, my fist plunging into his face. There's outraged gasps around me as Bering falls to the floor.

"I told you that's not a way to treat a lady," I say through gritted teeth. Bering sputters some threatening nonsense, but I don't care.

"Are you ok?" I turn toward Bianca to ask, and she gives me a soft nod, her big, luminous eyes wide as she's looking at me as if I'm her knight in shining armor.

"Let's not get too ahead of ourselves." Martin gets up, coming around to check on Bering. "I'm sure Anthony here only meant well." I frown at his words, and a glance at Bianca tells me I should drop it. I didn't realize her father was so callous to her — his own child. But Martin being Martin . . . It doesn't surprise me. It just makes me feel even worse for her. What is her life even like, having a self-serving narcissist for a father? He clearly doesn't care about her.

"If you'll excuse me," I say rather tersely and take my leave before I do something worse. I already feel bad for leaving Bianca there, an innocent lamb for their slaughter, but I need to realize she's not my concern.

You just met her!

My brain is telling me to drop it, but my heart . . .

Fuck!

I'm almost in the driveway when someone calls out my name. I stop and turn. Bianca is running toward me, her long skirt hampering her movements.

"Mr. Hastings," she says, huffing out a breath as she reaches me.

"Are you ok? What happened?" I immediately ask, my previous thoughts promptly forgotten.

"I wanted to thank you. For what you did in there," she speaks softly, the corner of her mouth raising ever so slightly.

"You don't have to thank me. I did what anyone would have done."

"And yet you were the only one who did." She raises her head to look at me, and we stare at each other for a moment.

I lift my hand and I tug a stray strand of hair behind her ear, marveling at the softness of the texture.

"You shouldn't measure your worth by their words, Bianca."

"Thank you." She gives me another tremulous smile before dashing back toward the house.

I stare at her retreating figure and I know.

I'm in deep trouble.

Fuck!

For as long as I've been seeing Pink, we've never exchanged numbers or any personal details. We always scheduled our next meeting in the moment. Which is why I'm here. I will not stand her up, but I need to put a stop to our encounters.

I watch the door of the room open, and Pink struts in, her tits almost spilling out of her top. She drops her jacket to the floor and then she's on me.

"Pink," I say, stopping her hand from reaching for my crotch.

"What?" she pouts at me.

"We need to talk." My tone is different from usual, and I find that I'm not in the mood for any games.

"We can talk . . . and do other things." She smiles, her hand creeping up my thigh.

"No. That's exactly what I want to talk to you about. We can't do this anymore." I grab her hand, trying to put some distance between us.

"What do you mean?" She frowns, tilting her head to the side.

"I'm trying to pursue someone and it wouldn't be right . . ."

"Who?" She cuts me off, her voice holding an edge to it.

I raise an eyebrow at her. We'd agreed on no personal details.

"You don't need to know about it." My voice is impersonal as I say this, but it's better to end things on friendly terms. And going by her reaction, I sense some underlying jealousy.

I stand up and go for the door, but she grabs onto my hand.

"Why? What does she have that I don't?"

"Stop this," I say, disentangling myself from her. There went my attempt at a parting on good terms.

"No. You must tell me. Does she fuck you like I do?" She scowls, and the viciousness of her words leaves me speechless. Maybe I've given her false hope, but while our chemistry has always been amazing, that's all it's ever been. And I was clear from the beginning.

"Bye, Pink." I turn toward the door once more.

"Tell me!" She raises her voice. "Does she worship your cock like I do?" On her knees, her hands go to my fly. I swat them aside, locking her wrists above her head.

If I must be cruel, then so be it. At least she'll understand that it's over.

"No, but that's just the thing. She's too pure and

innocent for that." I push her aside and leave. I can still hear her screams behind me, and I shake my head.

Maybe it is my fault. Maybe I gave her too much attention with our weekly meetings, and she imagined there would be more to our affair. It was just fucking. Savage, out of this world fucking, but it was just fucking.

This woman, though, the one that's been haunting my dreams?

She's my future wife.

CHAPTER
Six

BIANCA

I'D GONE through the worst torment of my life in the last few weeks. So wrecked with worry I'd been that Theo had fallen in love with someone that I could barely sleep. I'd resorted to keeping myself awake by sniffing more and more white powder, all the while checking all surveillance devices I'd placed on his person.

But nothing happened. He never met with anyone.

My paranoia was getting the best of me, and I simply could not focus on anything else but Theo's mystery woman. Who was she? How was she better than me?

Most importantly, how do I kill her?

One late afternoon, I am going through one report that my P.I. had compiled on Theo. So focused I am on what I'm doing that I barely pay any attention to the notice that someone is asking to see me. I absentmindedly think it must be Drew.

Ever since I've become more independent, he'd started stepping back from his duties and had even married last year. Now, he mostly works remotely if I have any assignments for him. He's also the perfect alibi when my father decides to show some interest in what I'mdoing.

I head downstairs, and to the drawing room, expecting to see Drew. Instead, I'm more than surprised when it's Theo who is waiting inside the room, his back to the entrance.

I carefully step inside, suddenly alert and curious to the reason for his visit.

"Bianca." He turns, offering me half a smile. I reciprocate, putting on my best act.

"Mr. Hastings." I greet him back, still addressing him formally.

"Call me Theo, please," he says, motioning me to the settees.

"Theo." I settle on the couch next to him but still keep an appropriate distance — even if it's killing me. My nostrils are flaring ever so slightly as I take in the scent of him, his nearness, both of which I'd missed so agonizingly much over the last few weeks.

"What brings you here?" I ask, schooling my features to reflect my confusion at his presence when all I want is to jump his bones, tell him to take me right here.

"I wanted to make sure you're ok. After last time . . ." he pauses, "I hope nothing happened after I left." His concern floors me, but then I realize what this is all about.

I'm just a battered woman to him, someone in need of saving. So he's taken it upon himself to make sure I am ok. If I didn't know this was Theo's nature — to save everyone — I might have been hopeful at his inquiry. But as it stands, I can see that I am just another pet project for him.

From reading his file and following his daily life, I'd drawn some conclusions about what makes Theodore Hastings the man he is — his humanity. He simply can't help himself when he sees anyone in trouble, offering to help even if it might be to his disadvantage. He's simply that good, the opposite of me.

But then I realize that this might be to my advantage. Maybe playing the victim is exactly how I can ensnare him.

I look down, and I fidget.

"I'm fine," I say, making sure my voice trembles a little. As expected, he picks up on my distress immediately, and he takes my hands into his. I almost sigh out of pleasure from that contact alone.

"You can tell me if something happened. I don't think I mentioned this last time, but I work with the NYPD." He's clasping my hands, as if to reassure me. I turn my head to the side, a whimper escaping my lips.

"It's nothing I'm not used to," I finally admit, looking

at him from the corner of my eyes to gauge his reaction. His eyes widen slightly.

"It's happened before?" he asks as if it's hard for him to hear this, so I just softly nod.

"Goddamn it!" he curses.

"I'm so sorry, Bianca. I'll have a talk with your father." The moment he mentions my father, I vigorously shake my head.

"No. Please. Don't mention it to my father . . ." I keep shaking my head, molding my lips in a thin line to reflect both fear and reluctance.

"But . . ."

"Please, you'll only make it worse." I beg him.

"Then what can I do?"

"You don't have to do anything. It's not your problem."

"I want to," he continues, his expression grim.

"It's fine, really." I stand up, my back to him. Taking a deep breath, I put on the best act of my life.

"You should go, Mr. Hastings."

I don't even turn to see how he might react to this. I just continue what I already started.

"You'll only get me in trouble with my father. He doesn't like me to entertain strange men."

He doesn't speak for a moment, and I have to wonder if I went too far with my rejection.

"I'm sorry you don't feel safe enough to talk to me," he says, his tone defeated.

I don't look back as I leave the room, still debating whether I'm doing the right thing. I'm literally banking on Theo's savior syndrome.

Prove me right, Theo!

The following days turn into weeks and into months. Theo proves to be as relentless as I'd pegged him. Every so often, he would come to check up on me, finding some sort of excuse to question whether I feel unsafe or if anything else happened to me. He's sweet that way. But even though his visits are quite frequent, it isn't enough anymore. Especially with this mystery woman he'd left Pink for still unknown.

I bite on my pen, trying to figure out what to do next. Sure, I'd appealed to his protective instincts, and he'd taken the bait, coming to see me almost weekly. Still, I need more. I need him to see me in a romantic light.

As I keep on thinking how to turn our relationship around, one of the staff announces that I have a visitor. I go down the stairs a little too fast, deep down hoping it will be Theo.

I'm not disappointed as I see him in the foyer, all dressed up in a suit and flowers in his hand. He looks a little uncertain as his gaze roams around until it settles on me.

"Theo?" I ask, coming to stand on the same level as him.

"B, hi." He gives me a lopsided smile, thrusting the flowers in my direction. "For you."

I frown. "With what occasion?"

"I wanted to talk to you about something, if that's ok," he replies instead, leading me toward the garden.

"What is it?"

During his visits in the last few months, we'd engaged in some small talk and we'd gotten to know each other better. Well, he'd gotten to know Bianca Ashby. I already knew all there was to know about him.

"I know we haven't known each other that long but . . ." He trails off, bringing his hand up to scratch the back of his head.

"I talked to your father, and I asked permission to court you," he blurts out suddenly, and my eyes widen. What? "If you're agreeable, that is," he amends.

"You're asking to date me?" I ask him to clarify, because really, this was the last thing I would have imagined he would say. A spark lights itself within my heart, and I get the urge to smile like a fool — but I know I can't. I need to keep my ruse.

"I know this is rather out of the blue. I've esteemed you for a long time now, but I was trying to give you space to get used to me since I know you've never dated before," he adds, almost apologetic.

"You like me?" I must sound like a broken record, but I need him to spell it out for me so I can throw an inner party and finally plan our future wedding.

"Yes." He nods, and tucking a strand of hair behind my ear, he gives me the most gorgeous smile. I almost swoon, but not quite, since I need to keep up my shy girl image. I lower my head and blush.

"I'd like that very much," I tell him, probably the only honest thing I've ever told him. "You said my father approves?"

"He'd given me permission a few months ago, but it was my prerogative to take it slow. I don't want you to feel pressured in any way to say yes to me . . ."

"No, no," I say, rather quickly. "I'm not pressured. I like you too," I admit, lowering my gaze.

I watch from under my lashes as a wide smile spreads across his face.

"I'm curious," I start, still not looking at him. "Since when have you liked me?"

"Since I first saw you," he answers solemnly and I hold my breath. It can't be, can it?

I wreck my brain for the dates and realize he broke it off with Pink after that disastrous lunch. Is it possible I was the mysterious woman all along? I suddenly want to laugh at the absurdity of it all.

I was jealous of myself.

I school my features, centering my thoughts on the present. I slowly lift my head to gaze at him bashfully.

"I'm glad," I whisper.

Maybe not all is lost.

I put in a lot of effort for our first date. After spending hours shopping and watching different tutorials to learn how to comport myself, I feel like I am finally ready.

I'd chosen a black dress that, while modest, still emphasized my curves and drew eyes to my cleavage. Theo needs to be reminded that while I am a sweet, gentle woman, I am still a sexual being and his thoughts should be focused on that. He should yearn for me, but not get me. This is all about building that anticipation that will make him mine in the end.

I slip my feet into a pair of sandals and I head downstairs.

Theo is already waiting for me, looking as sleek as always. Taking advantage of the fact that he has not noticed me yet, I let my gaze roam greedily over his figure. He is so decidedly attractive that I feel myself growing wet just gazing at him. All these months of celibacy haven't done me any good, and I'm one step away from pouncing on him.

He suddenly turns, his eyes roving over my body, the darkening of his irises a good indication that he likes what he sees. By now, I'm quite familiar with Theo's cues, especially his sexual ones. And I know he's one step away from ravishing me, too.

Oh, if only he would . . .

"You look exquisite," he rasps, and I give him a shy smile and a blush.

"Thank you. You too."

He offers me his hand, taking me to a cab and then to our restaurant. I can tell he's put a lot of thought into this. The entire setting is intimate and romantic. We are led to a small alcove, and we both take our seats.

"This is lovely." I add, trying to break the awkward silence. I look up slightly to see Theo staring at me intently. I frown.

"Do I have something on my face?" I ask, afraid I'd smeared some lipstick.

"No." He shakes his head, half-amused, but he doesn't continue.

The server comes around to bring us water and hand us the menu. Theo's eyes narrow as he follows the server's movements. It's only when the server leaves that Theo returns to normal. Odd.

He turns his attention back to me and smiles.

"What are your plans after graduation?" he asks, and I internally smirk. This is what I was waiting for. I'd prepared for this, and I have the perfect answer for anything he might ask.

On the outside, I school my features to convey uncertainty as I start my rehearsed speech.

"I've been thinking about a project . . ." I trail off, "but I don't know if I can do it."

"Of course, you can. What is it?" He reaches across the table to put his hand on top of mine and I soak in the contact, almost moaning at the feel of his skin on mine.

"I want to start a foundation for the less fortunate. I've put together a business plan, but I don't think my father is going to allow me." I lower my gaze as I whisper. "He doesn't like women working." I watch from the corner of my eye as Theo grits his teeth, that statement having the desired effect on him.

"I can talk to him. If you want to do it, you will." He squeezes my hand and I purr in satisfaction.

"Thank you . . . thank you." I return the touch, trying to convey my gratitude.

"None of that. I want you to know I don't hold the same views as your father. While we may know each other in a professional capacity, I don't subscribe to his way of thinking."

"I know. You're a good man," I say and blush. His eyes crinkle at the corners, and he continues.

"What about family? Do you see marriage in your future? Children?" He goes straight to the point, doesn't he? I'd already accounted for that, seeing that Theo is quite traditional in that respect.

"I'd like that. As an only child, I've always wanted a

big family. Children . . ." I smile, "I'd like children." The corners of his mouth pull up and I can see he's satisfied with my answer.

The server comes again and places the dishes in front of us. He lingers a little more than necessary in front of me, and I frown. Following the server's line of sight, I see he's a little too entranced by my cleavage. Damn! I wanted to go for classy, not trampy. I'm unsure how to react, since my usual go-to would be to beat the shit out of him, but I can't do that with Theo in front of me.

"Eyes on me, kiddo." Theo suddenly interjects and the waiter flinches. Theo narrows his eyes at his name tag, "Owen," he starts, "I'm not a very forgiving man, especially when it comes to this lady." The threat in his tone was clear and Owen starts shaking his head while mumbling an apology. Theo only raises an eyebrow at him, and Owen immediately scurries back to the staff room.

"You didn't need to be so harsh," I say softly, trying to ease the tension I sense in him.

"You're too naïve, little one. If you knew what he was thinking . . ." He shakes his head. "He needed to know you're off limits."

"I am?" My mouth opens just a fraction, looking at him in wonder.

"You are." He smiles confidently. "When you agreed to date me, you agreed to be mine. And I don't share."

Good. Neither do I.

But I don't voice that. No, I just look away, releasing a soft giggle and pretending to be embarrassed by his words.

We spend the rest of the date discussing various topics, and while I'd prepared an entire list of answers to give him, I find that we do have a lot of things in common, like our stances on politics, religion and social reform.

As the end of the night nears, I instantly get giddy about the thought of him kissing me. The cab drops us at my home and I turn to him, looking expectantly.

"I had a great time," I say, the intensity of his eyes sending a shiver down my back. Yes, this is the moment.

He comes closer, his hand reaching out and caressing my cheek.

"Me too, little one. I'll see you next week." He leans in for the kiss and I close my eyes, my lips ready to meet his.

But they don't.

Because he doesn't kiss my lips.

He barely grazes my forehead.

"Goodnight," he says, and then he's gone.

What? No kiss? Where is my kiss?

I'm left flabbergasted, looking at the spot he's just vacated, and I realize something. Maybe my shy girl pretense is backfiring. At this rate, will he ever touch me?

Shit!

I go straight to my room and I dial Vlad. I know what I have to do; I just need a little something to push him.

"Vlad," I say the moment he picks up, "I need you to hire someone to attack us. I need it to be perfect." I start explaining what I need the attacker to do: scare me enough that I'll need to be consoled. Theo would, of course, save the day, and then he would have to comfort me. Ravaged by anxiety and in his arms, the entire scene would end in my much-desired kiss.

"Slow down," he drawls, "you want me to pay someone to attack you just so your suit can save you? You're crazy."

"I'm not. Think about it! The intensity of the situation will make our endorphins run high, and one thing will lead to another and then . . ."

"Yeah, I got that, but really B? That's your master plan?"

"He kissed my forehead tonight. My forehead." I try to emphasize the gravity of the situation. "What if he doesn't think of me sexually? No, I can't have that happen."

"B," he groans, and I can tell he's going to object more.

"I swear if I don't get any action soon, my lips will wither and fall off. You wouldn't want that, would you?"

"I'm not sure that's biologically possible, but have it

your way. I'll find someone. If it backfires, it's on you, but don't say I didn't warn you."

"You're the best," I exclaim and send him a virtual kiss.

My plan will work. All my plans do.

CHAPTER
Seven

THEO

FOR THE MILLIONTH TIME TODAY, I stare at her, my eyes zoning in on her lips.

Fuck! Why did I decide to be such a gentleman?

But then I remind myself that she's never dated before, and I don't want to pressure her to do anything she might not be ready for. Just last time, she confessed that she's never kissed anyone before.

The thought of being her first, in every way possible, fills me with such possessiveness that I never want to let her go. I already have enough trouble letting her go when our dates come to an end.

I want nothing more than to kidnap her and have my way with her.

God!

I groan internally, shocked at the direction of my thoughts. I can't let my baser instincts ruin this for me. I don't want to scare her with my desires, especially when she's barely become comfortable being alone with me outside her house. I need to push everything down, and just focus on the present — on her.

"Have you decided?" I ask when she puts down the menu.

After our first date, I'd tried my best not to overwhelm her, but I just couldn't stay away. I'd dropped by her house the next day and I'd invited her to breakfast. And so a routine had developed. I could not get enough of her. She was like a breath of fresh air with her artless manner and her sunny disposition . And when I looked into those huge, gorgeous eyes of hers, I felt at home.

Especially after a long week at work, these Saturdays together were all I could think of.

"I'll have the omelet," she replies, giving me one of those sweet smiles I've come to crave more than anything.

Who would have thought I would ever find myself in this position? I'd never imagined I would one day consider a future with someone, not with my promise to my parents still fresh in my mind.

But I find that I can't choose one. I'll get my revenge, eventually. But Bianca . . . I want her by my side when that happens.

"I'll have the same," I add.

"I'll quickly go to the restroom before our orders

come." She gets up and heads to the back of the restaurant.

I pull up my phone and go through some messages when suddenly a noise gets my attention. People gasping around, I look up to see Bianca slowly approaching, shoulders slumped, gaze alarmed. Behind her is a man ordering directives as he waves a knife around, settling on her neck.

For a second, I stiffen, panic unlike anything I'd experienced before settling deep in my gut. But realizing the seriousness of the matter, I force myself to focus.

I stand, putting my hands up to show I'm unarmed.

"Easy," I start, taking a step forward. "That's my girl-friend you're holding." I catch Bianca's eye and I can see she is terrified but trying to hold it together. "Let her go, please."

"No!" he shouts, the hand holding the knife trem-bling slightly and digging into her flesh. God, I think I see some red. "It's all your fault! All of you!"

Alarmed at the possibility that he might actually harm her, I take a deep breath and decide to de-escalate.

"Easy. Maybe I can help you. What's your name?"

His eyes move swiftly from side to side, and for a moment I contemplate he might be on narcotics — that would make the situation even more unpredictable.

"Jacob . . ." he mumbles, looking anywhere but at me.

"Jacob, tell me what I can do to help you," I slow my words, trying to make him see me as inoffensive.

"You can't! No one can!" He flails his arm around, his knife now pointing toward me. Seeing that it's no longer at Bianca's throat, I release a relieved sigh.

"Maybe I can. Why don't you tell me about it?" I continue, while signaling to Bianca to make a run for it if she has the chance.

"It's all your fault, fucking elitists. If it weren't for you, I wouldn't have lost my job or ended up on the streets. My wife left me." He sniffles a sob. "She took the kids."

"She made a mistake. You can always turn your life around. Then you can get your wife and kids back," I say and watch the emotions play on his face. Just when I think I've gotten through to him, he tightens his hold on Bianca, placing the knife at her neck again.

"Look, man, there's still a chance to make this right. But if you continue with this . . ." I shake my head. "Then there's no returning, do you get me?" My eyes are fixed on Bianca the whole time, and I think of all the ways I can get her out of harm's way.

"But you don't get me. You don't know what it's like to be me!" His voice is even louder now, and I can tell he's becoming more agitated. Not good.

"Look, why don't you take me instead of her? I work for the police, I'm of more value to you." I hope he'll buy that. He looks at me with an angry expression, but he seems to consider it.

"Fine! But come slowly, or she gets hurt." I do as he

says, and he pushes Bianca to the floor just as I am one foot away. Seeing that she's out of his reach, I act. I go straight for the hand that holds the knife, knocking the weapon out and twisting his hand behind his back.

Using my knee, I kick his leg and hold him down on the ground, immobilized. He's thrashing in my hold, but he won't be able to escape anytime soon.

The police soon make their appearance and they take Jacob into custody. As soon as I am able to, I rush to Bianca's side. She's being treated by the paramedics for her cut.

"Are you ok?" I take her face in my hands, trying to gauge what she's feeling. God, she must have been so scared. "I'm so sorry." I tug her to me and hug her tightly, mad with myself that I put her in danger's way.

"Y-y-yes," she stammers, her small body trembling with residual fear.

"Shh, I got you." I kiss the top of her head, and I stroke her hair. Her hands come around my waist and she holds onto me.

"Thank you," she whispers, burrowing her face deeper in my chest.

When we get back to her house a while later, I feel reluctant leaving her alone, the sight of her so vulnerable, a knife digging in her neck still engraved in my mind.

I hold on to her hand, wanting to feel her warmth, her physical presence.

"You scared me, little one," I admit. She raises her enormous eyes to look at me and my restraint snaps.

Tugging her chin up, I lower my head and brush my lips across hers in the softest caress. She seems surprised, and a sigh escapes her. I part my lips slightly, and she follows my lead, her mouth opening under mine, her tongue probing hesitantly. The first contact sends shivers down my spine, the connection instantaneous.

I growl low in my throat as I deepen the kiss, holding her closer. Her hands brush over my arms, before settling on my face, trailing soft touches all over.

Suddenly, I take a step back, breaking the kiss. I need to put a stop to this before it goes too far — before I scare her with my passion.

Her eyes are glazed with desire, her hair mussed, her mouth oh-so-very well-kissed.

My thumb grazes her swollen lips, and satisfaction fills me to the brim.

She's mine!

"Good night, B," I tell her, turning around and leaving.

God, I really need to learn some self-restraint.

After the hostage incident, things change, and not for the better. I can barely stand being apart from her, and I'm afraid my overprotectiveness may stifle her. Wherever she goes, I go. It's as simple as that. I might have even gone a little overboard, as I'd taken advantage of my vacation days to shadow her.

I must have it bad if even work doesn't matter anymore.

Her classes? I'm in the back.

Her internship? I'm waiting around.

Her home? I'm a constant visitor.

Luckily, Martin isn't around all that much or that would have been awkward. But Bianca hasn't said anything. She seems to enjoy my presence as much as I do hers.

It's only after one month that she pulls me aside and tells me she's worried for me.

"Don't get me wrong," she starts, her eyes darting around, "I love having you with me everywhere I go, but I don't think your boss is going to be impressed with your absences."

I purse my lips, realizing where this is going. I'd been entirely too wrapped up in her that my job has come second.

"I know . . ." She puts a hand up to stop me.

"Please don't jeopardize your career because of me. I'm fine, I'm safe, I'm not in danger."

I nod reluctantly.

"I'm sorry I've been crowding you this past month," I apologize, hoping she isn't thinking of breaking up because of my overbearing ways. Because that is simply something that I will not allow.

"You don't have to apologize, Theo. I was just as scared as you, but the danger's already gone." She takes a deep breath, and I brace myself, mentally preparing all the arguments for why she should continue to date me. "I'm just worried they will fire you if you keep this up."

"Don't worry about that. I've never used my vacation days before, so I had plenty." I assure her. "But I hear you. I'll try to be more moderate. But for my peace of mind," I pause, thinking how to say this so she won't think I'm too controlling, "I'd like you to update me often throughout the day." I refrain from saying what I'd actually like — hourly updates. God, what am I turning into?

She gives me a smile. "Deal." On her tiptoes, she jumps up to kiss my cheek.

Damn! And that's exactly what I live for.

CHAPTER
Eight
BIANCA

"YOU GOT what you asked for, didn't you? Hastings sure is devoted to you now. A bit too much for my taste, I might add." Vlad lounges in his chair across from me, an amused expression on his face.

After the attack, Theo hadn't left my side — not even for one moment. Not that I'm complaining, if I'm being honest, since it's all I've ever wanted, but it's made doing my job a little hard. I've had to refuse two assignments in that time, and I'd had to limit my coke intake to once a week — if I was lucky. I'd noticed the signs of withdrawal immediately. I'd find myself restless and increasingly irascible.

Even though I'd wished for nothing more than to have Theo tied to me twenty-four seven, it's simply not possible with me leading a double life.

So, I'd had to gently nudge him toward considering

his career. He'd been quite receptive, so that issue was easily solved.

"I'm itching to land a kill." I ignore his jibe, taking out my precious baby — my Glock — and cleaning it.

"I might just have something." His smile grows and I have to narrow my eyes at him.

"Really?" I tilt my head, watching him suspiciously. After the last time, I don't think I'll trust him for a while. "You sent a fucking meth-head to attack us, so forgive me for not trusting your judgment." He could have sent anyone, not an unreliable, volcanic meth head that almost slit my throat.

"What are you talking about?" He furrows his brows, leaning forward. "Meth-head? That I sent?" he asks incredulously.

"You don't have to pretend you don't know what I'm talking about." I roll my eyes. "You could have sent someone less unpredictable."

"I didn't send anyone." He purses his lips. "At first I forgot and then Hastings seemed to come around so I didn't think it was necessary anymore."

"Are you fucking kidding me? You didn't send that guy?" Great! Simply great! I could have easily gotten killed because I'd been sure the guy would have never actually harmed me.

Fucking hell!

I don't even think as I lift my gun and shoot, the

bullet whizzing past Vlad's ear close enough to draw a droplet of blood.

He doesn't flinch.

Raising an eyebrow at me, he lifts his hand to pick up the blood with his fingers before bringing it to his mouth, licking it off.

"Is that war you're waging right now, little goddess?" He watches me intently, like a big cat on a prowl, ready to jump on its prey at any second.

"You fucking asshole. Do you realize I would have let that motherfucker slit my throat because I thought you hired him?" I stand up, pacing around and trying to calm myself.

Fuck!

"You suddenly care whether you live or die?" He smirks. "That's new."

"Asshole," I mutter under my breath.

He reclines in his chair, making himself more comfortable and seeming entirely unbothered.

"I may not have sent him, but it got you what you wanted, didn't it?" He shrugs.

"That's not the point," I grumble, but the annoyance is wearing off already.

"Just friendly advice. You should lock your suit down fast, before he finds out he's been awfully deceived. How long have you been dating now? A year? More?"

"It's not that easy," I mumble. Does he think I haven't

thought of that? I've been trying to give suggestions now and then, but Theo seems dense to all my attempts. I can't get the man to sleep with me, let alone propose.

I release a big sigh and plop myself back in my seat.

"He won't even go further than kissing. He sees me as this frail woman that he's afraid to offend if he's too forward."

"But isn't that what you wanted? Attract him by seeming innocent and shy? He already seems quite taken with you, though," Vlad suggests.

"Enough of that." I wave my hand dismissively, since I've done plenty of thinking on the subject myself, and it always leaves me frustrated. "Tell me about that kill. I need to blow off some steam."

More months of sitting around in the hell of sexual frustration, with Theo so close and yet so far. The most we'd done had been a heavy make-out session that had left both of us wanting. Damn him and his fucking misplaced honor. I've even tried to slyly make my way down his pants, but he'd stopped me, saying he doesn't think I'm ready for it.

I. Am. Fucking. Ready.

I am dying, that's how ready I am. It's been what, almost two years since he fucked me as Pink? I can't believe I've made it this long, but my breaking point is nearing.

I may just snap and tear his clothes off, but that would undo years of pretending to be sweet, innocent Bianca.

Fucking hell!

"It says here to add more rose oil," I say to myself as I follow the instructions for the love spell. When the natural cannot yield results, you have to reorient your-self towards the supernatural. Not that I'm a great believer, but at this point, I'm willing to try anything.

If I can't seduce him with my body, I doubt a dozen candles, some rose oil, and an incantation is going to do the job.

But alas, I will try it.

I place the candles in a circle and add some rose oil clock-wise as I recite the verses I'd found on the web.

"So mote it be," I end the chant, closing my eyes and willing it to happen. I imagine Theo on one knee, asking me to marry him, after which, he'd whisk me to bed and make love to me in a thousand ways.

A smile spreads on my face as I imagine it.

The spell done, I await the results.

Days pass, and then weeks, and I'm starting to

believe that either magic isn't real, or I must have offended those love fairies somehow.

But just as I feel hopelessness settle deep in my bones, I am regaled with the best of news — from my father, nonetheless.

One afternoon he calls me in his study to inform me that Theo's asked for my hand in marriage and that he will soon propose.

"You'll do better to accept, Bianca. You can't do better than him. He has a bright future ahead of him." My father lists all of Theo's qualities in an attempt to convince me that indeed, he is the best choice of husband.

On the surface, I nod like the obedient daughter that I am, but on the inside, I'm so giddy I high five all the love deities out there for making this happen.

I smile to myself. Now I just have to wait.

CHAPTER
Nine

THEO

TAKING A DEEP BREATH, I mentally go again over my lines. I need this to be perfect. I've already set up the bedroom. I'd taken to the internet for advice on the perfect proposal, and I'd followed all the advice I could find. From candles, to rose petals, and everything to ensure the atmosphere is as romantic as possible.

Bianca should arrive soon, and as I planned, I'll make her dinner first, and then I'll bring her to the room.

God, I'm too nervous!

We'd talked about our feelings before, but we haven't outrightly exchanged I love you's yet. But tonight is the night. I'll be handing her my heart on a platter.

The oven beeps, and I hurry to remove the tray. I start arranging the plates when the doorbell rings.

The moment I open the door, my jaw almost drops.

She looks like a goddess. My goddess.

She's wearing a dusty pink dress that clings to her body, emphasizing her hips and waist. I swallow hard, the sight of her looking so delicious doing little to calm my nerves.

I open my door wider for her, and she gives me a smile as she walks past me, waving a wine bottle. My eyes follow her around, almost glued to her ass.

"You cooked?" She places the bottle on the table, looking around the kitchen.

"Only for you." I come behind her, hands on her hips, and I lay a kiss on her cheek.

"You have to tell me what the occasion is." She sits daintily on the chair, and I stifle a groan, the sight of her enough to make me hard for days.

"You'll find out." I wink at her and proceed to serve dinner. Opening the bottle of wine, I pour it in our glasses.

"You're finally of age to drink," I add, amused. Sometimes it's easy to forget our age difference, since Bianca has a maturity beyond her years. Maybe I'd been a little reluctant to pursue her in the beginning because I'd thought her too young, but I was just biding my time and fooling myself in the process.

Ours is a matter of eventuality. It had taken me one look at her to know she was mine, a little longer to convince myself to go after her, and a hell of a lot longer to court her. But I know she feels the same as I do. It's in her slight shiver as I touch her, or the light inflection of her voice after I kiss her.

And tonight, she'll know just how much I love her.

We chat about her week. Since graduation, she's been working hard to put together a foundation against homelessness, and her project is picking up speed. I'd told her she could do it, and I made sure to support her at every point. I know how important it is for her to do this well, especially since her father seems to be against her working.

Tipping the glass to my lips, my eyes are on her, taking in her beauty — both inner and outer, and I wonder how I'm so lucky.

Out of everyone else in this world, she's mine and mine alone.

After we're done eating, we wash the dishes together, and I finally get the courage to ask her to the room.

"I have something for you," I tell her, leading her to my bedroom. Before opening the door, I put my hands to her eyes, steering her to the center of the room, so she's standing right in front of the strewn rose petals.

"What's this, Theo?" She giggles softly, and I can't help myself. I lower my lips to her pulse, skimming the sensitive skin toward her ear before whispering.

"Keep your eyes closed."

I move around so I can face her, and taking out the ring box, I prompt her to open her eyes.

When she does, it's to see me on one knee, ring out, in front of a row of roses that spells out Will You Marry Me?

She gasps, bringing her hand to her mouth, the corner of her eyes full with unshed tears.

"Bianca Ashby, will you do me the honor of becoming my wife?" I ask officially, and she jumps on me, tackling me to the floor.

"Yes! Yes!" she cries. "A thousand times, yes!" She brings her arms around my neck, holding onto me tight. "I love you, Theo." She whispers in my hair, and I feel my heart stop.

Fuck!

If this isn't true happiness, then I don't know what is.

"I love you too, B. So damn much it hurts," I confess, turning her so I can pepper kisses all over her sweet face. "So much."

Taking the ring out, I slide it up her finger — the perfect fit.

"It's gorgeous, Theo," she says in awe, her mouth slightly agape, her eyes shining with unshed tears. "Thank you."

"Only for you, little one. Only for you."

The candles are bathing the room in light, and her face looks even lovelier. I raise my hand to tuck a stray strand of hair, lingering on her cheek. I'd like nothing more than to throw her on the bed and take her hard and fast. It's not as if I haven't dreamed about that every single night since I met her. But I can't do that. I need to control myself and make her first time special.

But first, I have to make sure she's ready for it. If she's not, then I'll wait for as long as she needs, even if that means I'll be jacking off twice as much.

I move at the same time as she does, and we meet in the middle, our lips slowly caressing each other. I sneak my hand around her waist, bringing her into me and deepening the kiss.

"B . . ." I whisper, breaking apart for a second. "Are you . . ." I trail off, not knowing how to approach this so she doesn't feel pressured.

"Yes, please," she says shyly, backing up just enough so she can slide the zipper of her dress down and slip it down her shoulders. "I want you, Theo. I want all of you." She's now wearing only her bra and her panties, and I groan out loud at the sight. I don't even think as I scoop her in my arms, and take her to the bed, slowly lowering her on to the mattress.

She's unsure as she tries to cover her exposed skin, and I'm once again reminded that this is new to her, and I need to let her set the pace.

I pull my shirt off and throw it on the floor. Her eyes move greedily over my torso and I'm suddenly glad of my gym schedule. I want her to find me as attractive as I find her.

"The pants?" she asks, her tone breathless. I happily

oblige her, leaving my boxer briefs on so I don't shock her.

I advance toward her and she licks her lips, looking up at me with that innocent gaze of her.

Fuck!

My cock is straining against the confines of my briefs, and I'm fairly sure she can see just how much I want her. But her eyes seem to focus on my face, as if she's making a conscious effort not to look down.

I take her face between my hands and I proceed to kiss her, nice and slow, enjoying the feel of her — mine for the taking.

Spreading her on the bed and fitting myself on top of her, I proceed to kiss every inch of her skin, wanting to show her just how much I love her, worship her. As I move lower, I snap her bra clasp open and tug it off her. Her hands immediately go to her breasts and she gulps loudly, looking to the side.

"I . . . I've never," she starts, her voice full of embarrassment.

"I know. I'll be gentle, I swear." She nods, turns slightly to look in my eyes.

"I'm on birth control. I . . . I wanted to be prepared," she admits, a blush appearing on her pretty cheeks.

"God, B!" I groan, the idea that she's been looking forward to this as much as me exciting me to no end. "I'm clean. I've always used condoms before, but it's been a long time," I confess, and her nose scrunches up, a sigh of disappointment escaping her. "Shh, little one." I caress her face. "I wish I waited too. If I knew I'd find you one day, I swear I wouldn't have touched another woman." I tell her honestly, because when I'm with her, nothing and no one else matters. She's my future, my everything.

She gives me a tremulous smile, her fingers coming to rest on my cheeks and then tracing my lips.

"I'm glad. You're the only one for me, Theo. Always." Her words floor and humble me, so I show her just how much she means to me.

I turn my attention back to her body, trailing wet kisses down her neck and toward her breasts before taking one nipple into my mouth. Her mouth forms an o, but she urges me on. I lick and suck, enjoying the myriad of emotions playing on her face. I need her to be as relaxed as possible, her pleasure my foremost goal. I'm not a small man, and for the first time, I'm afraid it might not be as pleasant for her as I know it will be for me.

I move lower, kissing her stomach before reaching her panties. Hooking my fingers through the band, I tug them down her legs, leaving her bare for my view. She tries to close her legs, but I place a finger on her mound, marveling at the softness of her skin.

"Clean shaven," I murmur, surprised.

"I thought you'd like it," her voice is small as she says this, so I quickly assure her I'd like her any way.

That she put effort into this, to please me, makes me even happier.

Settling myself between her legs, I inhale her scent, nuzzling her lips with my mouth before diving in for the first taste. I give her a long lick, and she stiffens against me before relaxing once more. Centering the tip of my tongue over her clit, I circle it in slow motions, making her writhe under me, her hands involuntarily seeking my hair. She clutches at my scalp, and I continue, sucking the nub and nibbling it with my teeth. Her moans permeate the air, and pride swells in my chest.

I'm the one giving her pleasure. I'm the one owning her.

I use my fingers to prepare her, feeling her soft tightness and the way she clenches at my digits. Soon, she crashes, her orgasm making her contract all around my fingers, her soft gasps making my dick even harder.

Fuck! I need to take this slow.

Moving up her body, I give her a languorous kiss, using my hands to push down my briefs.

"I'm told this might hurt a little, sweetheart," I tell her, already feeling bad I'm about to cause her pain. I'd read plenty of articles to prepare for this night, wanting everything to be perfect, and Bianca as ready as possible to prevent any discomfort.

"It's ok. It's you." She gives me one quick kiss on the lips before urging me to proceed. My hands on her ass, I settle in the v of her legs, my cock brushing ever so softly against the wetness of her pussy. A hiss escapes me at the contact, the promise of pleasure to come.

Taking my cock in one hand, I rub it against her pussy, coating it in her juices before I push the tip in. My eyes are on her face, checking for any sign of discomfort, but she's watching me just as intently, her mouth open on an unreleased moan.

I move forward inch by inch, letting her get used to my size. A small crease forms between her brows and I still.

"Does it hurt?" I ask immediately, concerned.

She shakes her head. "It's just new. But I like it." She angles her hips and I slide all the way in. I take a deep breath, now hoping I will last. Her raw heat is almost too much to bear, and I have to stop myself from coming then and there — from one thrust alone.

"God, B. You feel so good," I rasp against her face, my lips seeking hers. I wait until she's ready and when she gives me a nudge, I start moving again. My arms come around her and I hold her tightly to my chest, driving my cock in and out of her. Her breathing picks up, so I quicken my pace, needing her to come all over my cock.

"Theo," she cries, her nails scratching my back and winding tightly around my neck. "Love you."

"Love you, too, sweetheart. So. Damn. Much," I growl in between thrusts. Her mouth is on mine as her walls grip my cock tightly, spasming around me. She lets out a soft moan, and I follow her, spilling myself inside of her. Relishing the feeling of marking her as mine.

We stay like that for a moment before I withdraw, running to the bathroom to get a washcloth. When I return, I spot a few droplets of blood smeared on her thighs and on the sheet — the evidence of her innocence. I clean her carefully, and she gives me the most satisfied purr.

She's mine. She's finally mine.

And for the first time, we fall asleep together.

CHAPTER
Ten

BIANCA

"YOU SHOULD HAVE BEEN THERE." I say, in between bites of food. "The wedding was so dreamy. For once, Martin spared no expense." I close my eyes, remembering how beautiful everything had been, and how Theo had made me feel like a princess.

"And now you're a happily married woman," Vlad replies drily.

"Very much so. You should try it. I'm positively glowing."

"No thank you," he rolls his eyes at me before adding, "and shouldn't other people be telling you that? You're just praising yourself."

I shrug. "Your loss. Wedded bliss is amazing. I now get at least four orgasms every day." I add, just to see the disgust appear on Vlad's face.

"Ew, too many details, B."

"Not enough details," I reply evilly. "You should see the way he works his cock in and out . . ."

"B!" Vlad groans, putting his hands over his ears. You'd think that for all the gore he sees and causes, he'd be more open about human sexuality. Then again, Vlad is a different beast altogether. I wouldn't be surprised if he's never intimately touched a female before, or even a male. Not that I'd even find out if he had, since his private life is entirely too private.

"Fine, fine. I'll stop talking about my husband's gorgeous ten-inch cock," I say with a smirk as Vlad removes a knife from his jacket. "I'm stopping. For real this time." I hold my hands up.

"Good. We have a kill to take care of." He shakes his head, walking out on me.

"You had to do it." I curse under my breath, using the back of my hand to wipe the blood off. Fuck, I'm practically covered in this shit.

Vlad isn't faring much better. He's sitting on the floor

between the two corpses, both of which have been ripped to shreds. Jack the ripper could take some pointers from Vlad. He's thoroughly soaked in blood, his eyes glazed with whatever's come over him, his nostrils flaring at the scent of blood.

Whatever!

I'm fucking pissed. If there's one thing I hate about this killing business, it's getting messy and bloody. That's why I prefer my pistols and killing from a distance. Then I won't have to wash out caked-on blood.

Ew!

I take out a napkin and I wipe some of the mess that's on my face when my phone rings.

Theo!

"Hi, sweetheart." My voice immediately changes, and I silently signal to Vlad to shut it — not that he's paying any attention to me.

"Where are you, babe?" he asks me, and I'm already looking forward to seeing him at home.

"I'm at work, silly," I half-joke, since this is indeed during my work hours. I just have other people take care of my workload while I do my this work. I frown as I fish a piece of flesh from my hair.

Fucking hell!

I take it and throw it at Vlad.

"Really?" Theo asks, and I immediately assure him.

"Of course, you know it's work hours."

"Is that so? I think it slipped my mind," he adds, almost absentmindedly.

"I'll see you at home. Love you!" I hang up, throwing my phone in my bag.

"We need to clean this shit up. Now!" I direct Vlad, and he finally snaps out of his reverie.

CHAPTER
Eleven

THEO

I CHECK out the window shops, still undecided on what I should get. Our wedding anniversary is approaching and even though I have a surprise planned for her, I still want to get her a little something, so she knows she's constantly on my mind.

Knowing how much she enjoys her sweets, I stop by a confectionery shop and I get her a selection of her favorite candy.

To make the surprise even sweeter, I decide to drop by her work. At the front desk, I spot her secretary, Jessica.

"I'm here to see Bianca," I say and wait to be buzzed in.

"She's not in, Mr. Hastings," she gives me an apologetic smile.

"She's not?" I frown, wondering where she could be.

Shrugging, I take out my phone to call her. Maybe she's running some errands?

"Where are you, babe?" I ask as soon as she responds.

"I'm at work, silly," she answers, her voice having the usual sweet quality to it. But this time it grates me.

I tense, and I try to be as normal as possible in my reply.

"Really?" I drawl, a deep sense of worry mingled with disappointment settling in my stomach.

"Of course, you know it's work hours," she continues with her lie.

"Is that so? I think it slipped my mind," I quickly amend.

"I'll see you at home. Love you!" She blurts before ending the call.

I'm left staring at her office door, still unsure of what the hell happened. I ask Jessica not to tell Bianca I'd dropped by, insinuating it's a surprise. I walk out into the cool fall weather, my feet carrying me numbly toward my car. I'm not fine. Not even close.

My sweet, innocent wife just lied to me.

She effortlessly lied to my face.

B, what are you hiding?

"The final installment in Bianca and Theo's story is Morally Corrupt, available HERE!

If you enjoyed this book, please consider leaving a review. It would mean a lot to me!

SUBSCRIBE TO VERONICA'S NEWSLETTER

veronicalancet.com / subscribe